CUPID'S ARROW

When Gemma Armstrong finds herself involved in another of her friend Suzy's crazy schemes, life inevitably turns complicated — especially when Kane Fenton becomes an unexpected part of the plan. An award-winning actor/director, Kane is heart-stoppingly handsome. So why, Gemma wonders, does he seem so alone? Thrown together in unusual circumstances, Gemma comes to know the private man behind the public image. Together, fighting their tangled emotions, they uncover the shocking secrets of Kane's past.

*Books by Margaret McDonagh
in the Linford Romance Library:*

MARGARET McDONAGH

---◆---

CUPID'S ARROW

Complete and Unabridged

LINFORD
Leicester

First published in Great Britain in 1997

First Linford Edition
published 2001

British Library CIP Data

McDonagh, Margaret
  Cupid's arrow.—Large print ed.—
Linford romance library
1. Love stories
2. Large type books
I. Title
823.9'14 [F]

ISBN 0–7089–4574–0

Published by
F. A. Thorpe (Publishing)
Anstey, Leicestershire

Set by Words & Graphics Ltd.
Anstey, Leicestershire
Printed and bound in Great Britain by
T. J. International Ltd., Padstow, Cornwall

This book is printed on acid-free paper

To Jacqui for old memories
and old friendships. Hope you find
your dreams in Wales.

1

Kane Fenton stabbed a computer key with his index finger and stored the work he had completed.

He was hungry and he needed a shower, a shave and some sleep, he admitted, as he leaned back in his chair and stretched his cramped muscles.

He had been buried in this office over the Christmas holidays putting the finishing touches to a screenplay — an adaptation of a contemporary novel to which he owned the rights.

Kane knew it was good. He could feel in his bones that this was a winner, and he always trusted his instincts. He knew this business. With several major nominations behind him and one award for Best Director, he was riding the crest of success.

The script he had just completed was a story of murder and mystery with a teasing, will-they-won't-they romance. The female lead was a strong, feisty character. Funny, smart, gutsy, she would strike a chord, Kane knew. And pitted against her male sparring partner, a tough, cynical, street-wise detective, the public's imagination and interest would be captured.

He stretched his legs and propped them on the edge of his desk, his mind already imagining scenes and effects. He knew how he would shoot this film, how to create the images, the tension, the drama.

As always at the beginning of a new project, he was excited, that gut-tingling enthusiasm bringing a fire to his blood that was the most potent stimulant of all.

But there was a considerable amount of work to do before the cameras began to roll, and filming began.

He had a hand-picked team he liked to work with, some of the best people in the industry. While his production company was small, it was flourishing, and he was in control of his own destiny, making the films he wanted to make.

The people around him were gifted, dedicated, and prepared to work as hard as he was, with as much attention to the smallest detail. So far, he was as satisfied as he was ever likely to be at this stage of a project. And everyone who was anyone in the film industry knew how difficult Kane Fenton was to please.

He stifled a yawn and scanned through the many messages that had accumulated on his answer machine in the last few days. One in particular brought a dissatisfied scowl to his lean face.

The unwelcome news that his right-hand man had accepted an offer to work in America and would no longer be available was not the kind of thing he wanted to hear at the start of what he anticipated would be an exciting but frenetic year. With a muttered curse, Kane erased the tape and stood up.

The rest of the house felt cold and neglected after the enclosed warmth of his office. He glanced through the circular window in the hallway out towards the stretch of the River Thames that ran past his cottage. It looked bleak and inhospitable.

Stepping under the steaming shower, his mind had already turned to the problem of his assistant.

He needed a replacement sooner rather than later, someone who knew the business, who could access funding. Someone he could work with. Someone he could trust. Someone whose commitment and zeal matched their talent. But who?

Kane tipped his face to the water, enjoying the stinging barbs on his skin. Eyes closed, he ran through several names and discarded them all. Then suddenly he knew he had it — the obvious person.

Richard Morris.

There was a name from the past. Fresh-faced, eager and incredibly nervous, they had worked together on their first television programme more years ago than he cared to remember. Kane had seen then that Richard had both talent and character although since then, they had lost touch. He had not heard of Richard for some while and wondered if he was still working in television.

Stepping out of the shower, Kane pulled on a towelling robe and went back downstairs. He stopped in the kitchen long enough to make himself a cup of coffee, then went through to his office.

At his desk once more, he rummaged through his address cards until he found Richard's.

Picking up the receiver, he tapped out the number, sipping his drink as he waited for the call to be answered.

'Richard Morris,' a once-familiar voice responded.

'Richard, it's Kane Fenton.' He grinned at Richard's surprised exclamation. 'Is this a bad time? Are you busy?'

5

'As always. You only just caught me. I'm on the way out to a New Year bash. Have you got something on tonight yourself?'

'No. I have work to do.' Kane's smile faded.

'You haven't changed then,' Richard commented, humour in his voice. 'You always did work too hard, Kane. All work and no play . . .'

'I've heard that before.'

'It's been ages since we last spoke, Kane. You've made a real name for yourself since the days we started out together. What are you working on at the moment?'

'That's why I'm ringing. I have a proposition for you. Interested?'

'I could be. We could discuss it tomorrow.'

Kane did not have to consult his diary to know the Bank Holiday was empty of social engagements.

'What did you have in mind?'

'Lunch.' A pause followed, then Richard added with a laugh, 'You can meet my sister.'

'The legendary Suzy? You always told me how crazy she is, though I never actually had the pleasure of meeting her.'

'That's something else that hasn't changed. Actually, Kane, you could do me a bit of a favour. Suzy had this idea . . .'

Kane listened with growing incredulity as Richard outlined his sister's latest madcap scheme and the part Richard wanted Kane to play.

'You want me to do what? Are you serious?' he exclaimed when Richard had finished. Why on earth was he even considering getting involved? 'I suppose you are going to remind me I owe you a favour.'

'Come to lunch anyway. No strings.'

He should say no. He wanted to say no. But a tiny spark of devilish curiosity gripped him. And then he found himself writing down the details of the restaurant Richard named.

What harm would it do to go along? He could discuss his plans with

Richard, have a break from his solitary office, and meet the sister he had once heard so much about.

A relaxing Bank Holiday would give him a breather, and time to recharge both his enthusiasm and his batteries which were always drained at this time of year.

And it would make a change from spending the whole of the holiday period on his own, like he usually did.

★ ★ ★

An irritating noise began to permeate Gemma Armstrong's deep, much-needed sleep. She groaned and rolled over, but then something insistent dug into her ribs, prodding her to wakefulness.

'Rise and shine! Happy New Year!'

The noise was Suzy's voice, the digging in her ribs Suzy's fingers. Gemma fought the dual intrusion.

'Go away,' she grumbled, pulling the weighty duvet over her head.

Undaunted, Suzy plonked herself on the edge of the bed and gave Gemma a more determined shake.

'Come on, Gemma, you can't lie here all day.'

With a sigh, Gemma pushed against the duvet and emerged a few inches from the cocooning warmth. A frown of annoyance pulled at her neat brows.

She felt like she'd hardly been asleep at all. They had arrived home from a New Year celebration party at some unearthly hour of the morning, and when she had fallen into bed, she had looked forward to a lazy lie-in and a relaxing day before she had to return to work tomorrow.

'What time is it?' she grumbled, pushing wayward locks of long, wavy blonde hair away from her face. She eased herself up on the pillows and forced her heavy lids to open so she could attempt to focus her bleary gaze on her friend's impish face.

Suzy flashed an irrepressible grin.

'A little after nine.'

'In the morning?'

'Of course in the morning!'

Gemma gazed at her friend in horror. 'Since when were you ever up before lunch on a Bank Holiday?'

'Don't look so surprised! We have things to do.'

'What things?' Gemma asked with suspicion.

'New Year resolutions.'

'This sounds ominous. What are you up to now?'

Unabashed, Suzy grinned again, and handed over a mug of steaming tea. Gemma curled her fingers round the warm china. Perhaps the brew would wake her up sufficiently. She had no idea what had induced her housemate's uncharacteristic behaviour, but she suspected from years of experience that she was not going to like it.

'Suzy, just tell me what this is all about,' she begged after a moment, unable to stand the suspense.

'You and Andrew.'

Gemma nearly choked on a mouthful of tea.

'Excuse me?'

'Look, I know you've been crazy about him for as long as I can remember.'

'Hardly that,' Gemma said, knowing her protests weren't entirely honest.

Andrew Robertson had been in Gemma's life for as long as she could remember. The son of one of her father's oldest friends, Andrew was a friend, the brother she'd never had, and she had worshipped him since childhood.

Those feelings had blossomed into deep affection and love throughout her mid to late teens, but it was one-sided.

Andrew continued to treat her as the girl she had been, not the woman she had become.

To make the situation worse, while she loved Andrew, he had fallen for the exotic charms of a woman called Felicity. To Gemma's amazement, Felicity was reluctant to be caught which only proved to make Andrew all the more keen.

'There are loads of gorgeous men out there. I just can't understand why you insist on waiting for stuffy, old Andrew to notice you.'

'Suzy . . .'

'Well, what's he got that's so special?' Suzy asked with a derisive snort.

'I can't help what I feel for him.' Gemma sighed. 'My life is full and busy. So what if I don't want to settle for second best?'

'But why would you want to save yourself for him? You'll be old and boring before you know it.'

'Thanks very much,' Gemma responded dryly.

'You know what I mean.' Suzy puffed out her cheeks in frustration. 'I'm not saying Andrew's sophistication and good looks don't have an appeal, but he's so dull.'

'He is not!'

Suzy waved the indignant protest aside.

12

'But he wanders around art galleries in his lunch hour — what else would you call him?'

Half asleep and tired of the argument, Gemma shifted in the bed and set the half-empty mug of tea aside.

'So what has all this to do with your resolutions?' she asked with some trepidation.

'Well, if it's really Andrew you've set your heart on, its time we took steps,' Suzy explained, warming to her task.

Gemma's brow creased into an anxious frown.

'What do you mean?'

Suzy ran her fingers through her short, light auburn hair, her hazel eyes sparkling with endeavour.

'At twenty-five, I do not intend to allow you to spend any more time alone. We shall force Andrew's hand once and for all.'

'What are you talking about?'

'Project Andrew!' Suzy grinned engagingly. 'I have a plan.'

Gemma's heart sank.

'No. Now, Suzy, listen to me — '

'This is a brilliant idea. It has to work.'

'Sure. Like all your other ideas.'

Gemma stifled a sigh, experience of Suzy's plans bringing a knot of tension to her stomach.

She was always being drawn into Suzy's hare-brained schemes, and they always had the inevitable disastrous result.

She knew from the start it would end in tears, but somehow, Suzy's irrepressible and adventurous spirit always bettered her own steady judgement — with predictable consequences.

'Now,' Suzy explained with enthusiasm. 'We have to make Andrew jealous. If he sees you with another man, he's bound to take notice and realise what he's missing.'

'No, I — '

'A bit of healthy competition, that's what you need.'

'Suzy!' Gemma wanted to scream at her friend in frustration. 'I'm absolutely — '

'Quiet, stop interrupting.'

Gemma closed her mouth. There was no stopping Suzy when she was like this.

'I've worked out the perfect set-up. Andrew will be green with jealousy in no time at all.'

'He's only interested in Felicity.'

'Then we shall make him uninterested. He just needs a bit of gentle persuasion, that's all,' Suzy maintained matter-of-factly.

'So how do you suggest I do that? I don't think I could just pounce on the first man I see in the hope it makes Andrew jealous.'

'You don't have to,' Suzy explained, completely serious. 'I've already sorted all that out! Richard is asking a friend of his to do it.'

Gemma gazed at her friend, dumbfounded by this ridiculous idea.

'You can't be serious?' she challenged in a horrified whisper.

'Of course I'm serious! I've arranged everything.' She rose to her feet, smiled happily, and patted Gemma on the hand. 'Now, get up and get ready. We're meeting them for lunch at noon.'

'Absolutely not.'

'This will work,' Suzy reassured her. 'Don't worry, Gemma.'

When the door closed, Gemma groaned and buried herself beneath the duvet once more. Don't worry. Suzy's famous last words.

2

'I cannot believe I am here,' Gemma muttered under her breath as she sat across the secluded booth from Suzy whose attention was focused on the menu.

With a heavy sigh, she glanced around the interior of the restaurant section of the Tudor-style pub Suzy's brother Richard had selected, her anxiety apparent as she twisted a napkin. The place was busy despite the fact it was New Year's Day.

Gemma returned her gaze to Suzy, and an affectionate smile curved the bow of her mouth as she studied her friend's appearance.

Suzy had a peculiar and unique style of dress. Layers of clothes in her favourite colours of reds, oranges, purples and pinks, should have looked dreadful, and would have on anyone else, but somehow, Suzy managed to carry off her weird ensembles with panache.

Even the garish and ubiquitous hat that perched at a jaunty angle on her head looked like it was meant to be there.

The fine strands of short hair that peeped from beneath the brim had been through a range of colours over the years from pink to orange to silver. Now, the natural auburn had been allowed to return, and Gemma was glad. The true colouring emphasised the appeal of Suzy's delicate features far more effectively than any artifice.

Suzy was elfin-looking, her bright hazel eyes sparkling with mischief, her freckled nose tip-tilted, her mouth generous and smiling, her chin set with determination.

She was a loyal, funny, endearing, and sometimes exasperating friend, the best Gemma had ever had.

Suzy and her elder brother, Richard, were the children of wealthy, successful parents, their father head of a major conglomerate. Gemma's father was in the diplomatic service.

When Gemma was eleven, he had been posted from Hong Kong to South America and her parents had sent her back to England and secondary education at a renowned girls' school on the South Coast.

It was there she had met Suzy. From the first day they had become thick as thieves.

They were opposites, and yet their friendship had endured all these years because for all their differences. They understood and complemented each other.

Suzy's exuberance and self-confidence was a buttress to Gemma's more reticent nature, while her commonsense and more cautious judgement was a foil for Suzy's devil-may-care excesses.

After school they had taken separate flats in London. While Suzy had opted for excitement and an outlet for her artistic nature and accepted a job as an artist with a successful publishing company, Gemma had taken a steady career in estate agency work.

With Gemma's parents once more on a long stay abroad, Gemma had taken up residence in their house, a stucco-fronted, elegant building in central London. She had invited Suzy to share with her. It was an arrangement that suited them both and brought back memories of their time at school.

But this latest scheme of Suzy's was not one Gemma found amusing. She had to be insane to have allowed Suzy to talk her into coming to meet Richard and his friend for lunch. She wondered if the man knew what plan was afoot . . . and if he did, why would he want any part of it?

She glanced at Suzy's determined, blithesome expression and felt an all too familiar sinking feeling in the pit of her stomach.

'Well, I hope Richard's New Year resolution wasn't to improve his punctuality!' Suzy grinned, propping the menu back between the stainless steel salt and pepper shakers.

A faint fluttering of hope dawned within Gemma.

'Perhaps he won't come. Perhaps he couldn't find anyone foolish enough to take part in this charade.'

'Don't be so defeatist. I spoke to Richard this morning. They'll be here.'

'And who is this stooge he's bringing with him?'

'I don't know.' A small frown passed briefly across Suzy's face. 'Richard said they go back a long way. I'm sure he'll be game for a laugh.'

'That makes me feel a lot better.'

Suzy rushed to cover her mistake.

'I didn't mean you, just that he isn't some stuffy, out-of-work actor.'

'For someone who has no idea who he is you seem remarkably confident.' Gemma sighed with wry exasperation.

Suzy remained unperturbed.

'Everything will work out fine, you'll see. I . . . ' Her words trailed off as she looked at something in the direction of the doorway.

'Suzy?'

'This is unbelievable!'

Gemma couldn't remember ever seeing Suzy fazed, but she was now.

'What's the matter?'

Suzy swallowed, her eyes wide as she glanced at Gemma and back towards the door.

'Richard didn't say. But — but I never imagined this!' she exclaimed.

'Who is it?' Anxiety sent a shiver up Gemma's spine as she shifted in her seat in an attempt to discover why Suzy was in such an uncharacteristic fluster. She was even blushing! 'Suzy, for goodness' sake, tell me.'

Before her friend had the opportunity to put her out of her misery, Richard Morris arrived at the booth, a smile of devilment on his face.

'What's wrong, Suzy?' he greeted with amusement, planting a kiss on his sister's astonished face. 'Catching flies?'

He laughed as Suzy's mouth snapped

shut, affection in his hazel eyes as he turned to Gemma.

'Hi, Gem.'

'Hi, yourself.' She smiled, covering her growing anxiety as she returned his light kiss.

'Well, I hope you're ready for this!' Richard grinned as he stepped back, and the man who stood behind him came into her line of vision.

Gemma was not sure how she managed to smother her gasp of shock as she took her first look and instant recognition hit her. No wonder Suzy was thrown.

Her startled gaze swung to her still-silent friend, passed back across the smug amusement on Richard's face, to clash with a pair of watchful, mocha-brown eyes.

Tall, lean and incredibly handsome, Gemma discovered that Kane Fenton was more impressive and arresting in person than on the screen or in photographs. And heaven knew, she would not have thought that was possible.

His hair was dark blond. Well-shaped, it was thick, and brushed back from his face. His skin had a healthy glow despite it being the depths of a cold winter.

Beneath dark brows, those mysterious eyes held an enigmatic expression, and were fringed with long, dark lashes.

He had a firm jaw, not too square, and there was a tiny hint of a cleft in his chin. Gemma's gaze lingered on the shape of his lips. That mouth was altogether too distracting.

Being familiar with his image in no way prepared her for the reality of him. Here she was, mere feet away from the man whose picture had adorned the walls of countless female bedrooms the world over.

Kane Fenton had been one of the best young actors in the country. At the height of his success, with directors clamouring for his talents, and hordes of leading ladies fighting for the chance to play opposite him, Kane had turned his back on his acting career.

Newspaper reports had headlined the news that his main ambition was to be behind the camera, to write, produce and direct his own films. In the last few years, his work had been widely acclaimed, with awards and nominations galore.

He was also popular for using British technicians, companies and facilities.

Still dazed, Gemma attempted to recover some sense of balance. She watched as Kane turned his attention to Suzy, noting the flush that stained her friend's cheeks in response to Kane's smile and handshake.

'I'm glad to meet you, Suzy. I've heard a great deal about you.'

Suzy glowed at the warmth in Kane's velvet voice.

'I'm sorry to say that Richard has kept you a secret from me,' she complained with a pout.

'Are you surprised?' Richard murmured.

'Honestly, Richard!' Suzy exclaimed. 'Some brother you've turned out to be. Imagine keeping a friend like Kane under wraps.'

'And have you pestering me all the time to meet him? I'm not daft, Suzy!' Richard laughed.

As brother and sister bickered on, Gemma felt an irrational shiver sweep through her as Kane shifted his attention and that dark gaze locked on her once more.

'Gemma.'

The sound of her name, spoken by his warm, velvety voice, was like a caress.

On instinct, Gemma responded to his outstretched hand and felt a tingle of electricity as his fingers curled around hers, longer than was necessary for politeness. Too long!

Her hand looked delicate, her skin creamy, in the enclosing darkness of his. Disturbed by her heightened senses and her powerful reaction to this man, Gemma pulled her hand away.

Casually, Kane slid off his dark jacket and draped it over the side of the booth.

He pushed the sleeves of his dark-mulberry, aran jumper up to his elbows, revealing strong forearms, and slid into the booth beside her.

Gemma was glad that Richard sat next to Suzy because she was spared having to look directly across at Kane at any point. But the relief was short-lived as the effect of Kane's nearness began to unnerve her.

The space, which normally would have been cosy, was cramped. His thigh, encased in expensive, charcoal trousers, brushed against hers, and there was no space to retreat from him. He was earthy, masculine, disturbing. And it was not the fact that he was a well-known personality.

There was some innate quality about him, a magnetic presence, that was impossible to ignore.

Questions buzzed through Gemma's brain. What on earth was Kane doing here?

Surely he could not know of Suzy's ridiculous plan. No-one in their right mind would agree to such a charade, especially someone such as Kane Fenton.

For a brief moment, Gemma closed her eyes and wished she could wake up back in her warm, comfortable bed and discover none of this was happening.

She was having some crazy dream. She lifted her eyes. No. She was still here, Kane beside her, warm and disturbing and far too real.

She swallowed down a sudden wave of panic. This had to be some kind of joke. That was it, wasn't it? Suzy and Richard couldn't possibly be serious.

★   ★   ★

Kane was concerned at the heaviness he felt pressing on his chest. It felt as if an elephant had sat on him — metaphorically speaking. And was it only pure coincidence that this had happened at the same moment he had set eyes on Gemma Armstrong?

With customary self-discipline, he forced himself to ignore unwelcome thoughts, and turned his attention to

Suzy Morris instead. She was everything Richard had said and more.

He had been hard pressed not to stare at her open mouthed, overcome with the first impression of her weird outfit, the glaring colours, and that ridiculous hat jammed at a rakish angle on her head.

He had been taken aback by Gemma, Kane admitted with a frown, his concentration on his thoughts and not on Suzy's incessant chatter. After all he had heard from Richard, he had been expecting someone just like Suzy. But Gemma was as far from Suzy as it was possible to be.

Conscious of her beside him, of the teasing hint of her perfume, Kane resisted the temptation to turn his head and look at her. Or rather, resisted for a few seconds, and then gave in. He shifted in the booth, his leg brushed against hers as he angled sideways so he could watch her without being obvious about it.

She looked both chic and cosy in

cream-coloured jeans which she wore with a fleecy overshirt. The warm shade of mink brought depth to the creamy perfection of her skin.

According to Richard, Suzy's idea was intended to help Gemma attract someone called Andrew with whom she was smitten.

As far as he was concerned, Kane could not see Gemma being the kind of woman who would ever have trouble attracting a man. Quite the reverse, in fact.

As he watched her, Gemma smiled at the continuing banter between Richard and Suzy. She had a beautiful smile.

His gaze lingered far too long on the outline of her mouth that was brushed with a hint of warm, subtle gloss. The top lip was prettily bowed, the lower one full and sensuous.

An indrawn breath snagged in his throat as Gemma turned her head and caught him staring at her.

Their gazes locked. Confusion replaced the uncertainty in her eyes for a brief moment, the expression changing to shock and then anxiety. Even, white teeth nipped at the lower lip, betraying her nervousness, before she looked away.

The heaviness in Kane's chest settled in again. He leaned back in the booth and tried to remember how to breathe. He was very much afraid there was deep trouble in store if he was not careful.

Despite all his good intentions to keep his distance from Suzy's madcap plan and to use this lunch for the sole purpose of putting his proposal to Richard, Kane found himself intrigued, drawn deeper in than he had ever expected or wanted to be. Gemma Armstrong was too distracting by half.

3

Gemma watched with mounting dismay as both Suzy and Richard left the booth and went to the bar to order the drinks and food.

She had no recollection of examining the menu, nor of making any decisions as mundane as what she wanted to eat or drink. Her only awareness was that now she was alone with Kane.

Her insides knotted with nervous tension as she struggled to ignore the effect of his presence beside her. She could not think of a single, sensible thing to say to the man.

He had been looking at her ever since he had arrived. She had felt it, just as she could feel she was the subject of his inspection now. It was unsettling to say the least.

What on earth had Suzy landed her in this time?

As the electric silence stretched on, Gemma fidgeted uneasily on the seat and cast a wary glance at Kane, unnerved when her gaze clashed with his.

His eyes were dark, mysterious, watchful. Flustered, she twisted a strand of her hair round her finger before she offered him a tentative, apologetic smile.

'I'm sorry,' she began, controlling the waver and struggling to inject some normality into her voice. 'I can't imagine how you have been dragged into this.'

'I presume you have a strategy worked out?' he asked in that deep, mellow voice.

'Goodness, no, this is Suzy's ridiculous idea, not mine,' Gemma stressed, trying not to look directly into his eyes but not really managing.

A smile played around his mouth.

'Having met Suzy, I now believe Richard's tales are not exaggerated after all.'

'Exactly.' Gemma returned the smile, relief lifting a weight from her shoulders. 'I'm sure you agree it's best to forget the whole thing.'

'I didn't say that.'

Gemma's eyes widened as the impact of his words hit home. He couldn't be serious, surely? There was no way Kane could actually consider being part of such a ludicrous scheme.

'You are joking, yes?' Gemma prompted hopefully.

'No.'

'But why on earth would you even want to consider going along with such a thing?' Gemma protested, panic building inside her. 'What's in it for you?'

'That remains to be seen.'

His enigmatic response, delivered with maddening calm, tightened Gemma's stomach into knots. She took a steadying breath and delivered what she hoped was a composed smile.

'Look, Mr Fenton, I — '

'Kane,' he interjected smoothly, that

compelling voice and sultry gaze disturbing her train of thought.

'Kane.' Gemma struggled to remember what she had been going to say. 'Yes. This is not a good idea, Kane. You said yourself that you had heard of Suzy's outlandish schemes, and believe me, you really don't want to be involved.'

Kane leaned back and stretched his arm along the back of the booth.

'Perhaps there are benefits for me, too.'

'What benefits?' she queried, nervous and wary of the lazy way he had spoken, the speculative gleam in those dark, unfathomable eyes.

'If I help you out, you can help me.'

'Excuse me?' Gemma's eyes widened.

'There are a few functions that I am expected to attend, and no-one whom I'm keen to be with at the moment,' he explained. His dark gaze made a slow and disturbing pass over her, casual but intense, sending a tremor of unwanted awareness through her. 'Maybe you could fill that rôle for me.'

'I don't think so.' Gemma's denial was instantaneous.

'Why not?'

'Because . . . ' Gemma floundered as she watched amusement sparkle in the depths of his eyes and a ghost of a smile tilt his mouth. 'Why are you doing this? Why come here with Richard today?'

The amusement left his eyes and he watched her for a moment, a slight frown pulling at his brows as if he was searching for his own explanation.

'I need to talk to Richard about business. He suggested this lunch.'

'But he told you about me, about Suzy's plan,' she pressed.

'Some of it.' Kane dragged the fingers of one hand through his hair in a gesture of apparent impatience.

'So why not just accept that I don't want to do this?'

He studied her for a moment in silence, that glint of amusement back on his face.

'You intrigue me, Gemma.'

Flustered once more, Gemma glanced round for signs of Richard and Suzy returning. They were taking far too long. Suzy's doing, no doubt.

She was probably grilling Richard about Kane, and where he fitted in with her plan.

Gemma let out a small sigh of despair. She wished she was anywhere rather than trapped in this booth with Kane Fenton. Why couldn't Richard have found someone ordinary to bring to lunch?

There was something inevitable about the way Gemma's gaze was drawn back to Kane's. The dark eyes were watching her in a way she found too intimate.

It was as though he was reading her private thoughts, touching her soul. Despite her desire to do so, she seemed unable to look away.

She couldn't say how much time ticked by, if it was minutes or mere seconds that they watched each other in silence. The touch and control of his gaze was almost physical, she thought with a shiver. Eventually, she began to feel less tongue-tied.

'What did you mean? How could I intrigue you?' The questions came out more nervous-sounding than she had intended. 'You don't even know me.'

That little smile appeared again, playing around with the shape of his mouth in a way that was altogether too distracting.

'I know enough to wonder what it is about this Andrew that has you so infatuated.'

'I am not infatuated with Andrew,' Gemma snapped.

'No?' He raised one eyebrow. 'What would you call it?'

'Mr Fenton . . . Kane,' she amended. 'I don't know what you have heard, but I have known Andrew a long time. I know how I feel about him and it is not infatuation.'

He watched her, his expression unreadable.

'Hasn't it occurred to you that if Andrew was interested he would have made a move by now?'

'There is no need to make it sound so extraordinary that he could be interested,' Gemma was compelled to retort.

'On the contrary. The man must be an idiot. That's my point . . . and why I'm intrigued.' He propped an elbow on the table and rested his chin in his hand. 'Tell me why a beautiful and intelligent, young woman is wasting time waiting for one man when others must be queuing up to get your attention.'

'I beg your pardon?' she demanded, a frown creasing her brow at his words that sounded far too critical to her.

'Life isn't like it is in the movies, you know. Love doesn't always work out.'

A flash of temper flared inside her. She was not about to sit here and be psycho-analysed by a stranger, no matter who he was!

'Do you have to be so patronising? I am not stupid, nor do I believe in

39

fairytales, but I'm not a cynic like you.'

'I'm a realist, not a cynic,' he refuted mildly. 'I think you expect too much.'

'Then it's fortunate I am not interested in what you think. I've had plenty of boyfriends, but contrary to your opinion, I do not need a man in my life to make it complete.'

'You want Andrew.'

'My happiness is not dependent on Andrew or any man. I love Andrew. I don't expect anything. But I do want to see if there's a chance.'

Kane was silent for a long moment and she began to feel a fool for explaining anything at all to him. What business was it of his anyway? This was all Suzy's fault.

'Then we will.'

Lost in her thoughts, Gemma blinked at the sound of Kane's voice, confused as she digested his words.

'We will what?'

'See if there's a chance for you and Andrew.'

'No!' Panic returned to engulf her.

'There's no need for you to do this. I don't want — '

'I'll get your phone number from Richard and give you a call,' Kane interrupted, ignoring her protests.

She was about to object even more loudly when Kane released her gaze from the magnetic pull of his and glanced round. Gemma saw Suzy and Richard returning to the table with the drinks, and she scowled at the beaming grin on her friend's face.

This situation was getting out of hand, Gemma worried, conscious of Kane withdrawing his arm from the back of the seat and shifting his position. Dread welled inside her as she remembered the results of Suzy's other schemes.

Kane wouldn't call, she told herself. Of course he wouldn't. Now all she had to do was wait until the whole silly idea blew over.

But what if he did call? A thousand thoughts flashed into her head. What was she going to do?

* * *

He had to be crazy, Kane decided as he sat brooding in his office that evening. He hadn't done a scrap of work since he had arrived home, and all because he had been unable to get Gemma Armstrong's image out of his mind.

What was the matter with him? In his work, he was surrounded by attractive women. But he had never allowed any of them to get particularly close to him.

He thought back to lunch. Gemma had filled his mind, dominated all his senses. And after she and Suzy had left, he had struggled to put his proposal to Richard, his concentration shot to pieces.

Had Richard agreed to the offer, or had he asked for time to consider his situation?

Kane couldn't remember and that made him angry. He, Kane Fenton, renowned for the meticulous and efficient way in which he operated, had been completely caught out by a pretty woman.

If having his attention diverted by a pretty woman was all it was, that would be bad enough. But oh, no, he'd done better than that. Instead of being relieved and taking the easy way out Gemma had offered him, what had he done? Gone on to persuade her to agree to Suzy's ridiculous plan of all things.

Kane grimaced. Gemma had been even less pleased with the idea than he. So why had he set about involving himself?

Maybe Gemma's dogged reluctance to have anything to do with him had made him consider it, or maybe it was the many questions he had about her. She was an enigma. However much he tried to deny it, he wanted to find out more about her.

His first impression, aside from her beauty, had been of quietness and dignity. Her misty blue eyes were filled with a sharp intelligence, and she had shown an unexpected feisty side when he had riled her.

The more he thought about it, the more ridiculous the whole thing seemed. He wouldn't ring her, he decided with a frown. They could forget the whole business.

That's what Gemma wanted. It was what he wanted. He sat and stared at the telephone, at Gemma's number sitting beside it. He definitely wouldn't ring.

But as he sat for the next few minutes thinking of her sunny smile, her misty blue eyes and that tempting mouth, he found himself picking up the receiver.

★ ★ ★

'The man is gorgeous, Gemma!' Suzy enthused, lounging in the doorway of the kitchen. 'Fancy Richard knowing him and never letting on.'

'It's amazing,' Gemma said sarcastically.

'Don't be in such a mood!'

Gemma counted to ten and concentrated on making the hot chocolate. If she heard any more about Kane Fenton she was going to scream.

'Just think how much better this is,' Suzy continued, unperturbed. 'Andrew couldn't help but notice you going out with Kane.'

'I will not be going out with Kane,' Gemma stressed through gritted teeth, her patience at snapping point.

Suzy ignored her ill humour and laughed.

'It'll be fun. Imagine having Kane at your beck and call, whenever you want. I wish it was me.'

'Then you arrange to see him, if he rings, which he won't. Just forget it, Suzy.'

'You can't be that immune.'

Gemma sighed as she poured the chocolate drink into two mugs and set the pan in the sink to soak.

'This silly scheme of yours was to help me attract Andrew . . . supposedly. It's him I'm interested in.'

'I haven't forgotten, silly. But — '

'Suzy!' Gemma moderated her tone. 'I am not interested in Kane Fenton, I do not intend to go out with Kane Fenton and I hope I never hear of Kane Fenton ever again.'

She thrust the hot mug into Suzy's hands and stalked from the kitchen, her temper simmering inside her. She flopped down in a comfortable arm-chair in the sitting-room and drew her legs up beneath her.

What a day! She would be glad to return to work tomorrow and forget all about this New Year holiday. When the telephone rang, she reached out a hand for the receiver.

'Hello,' she snapped, without intending to.

'Gemma? It's Kane.' Her fingers tightened their grip on the receiver. Even over the phone his voice sent a ripple down her spine.

'Hello. I didn't expect to hear from you.'

'I know.'

There was a smile in his voice.

'Tell me some of the places we'd be likely to bump into Andrew.'

'Kane, I don't — '

'Come on, just tell me, Gemma.'

She ignored the smug, self-satisfied grin on Suzy's face and closed her eyes.

It felt as if everything was conspiring against her, and it didn't seem to matter that she didn't want to do this.

'Monday lunchtime he always goes to the Tate,' she told him, resignation dulling her voice. 'Wednesdays, it's his favourite restaurant, Friday nights the club, and then at the weekend, the opera, ballet or theatre.'

As she listed Andrew's routine, she realised how predictable it sounded.

'We'll have our first date on Wednesday at the restaurant,' Kane announced before she had the chance to protest. 'I'll pick you up at seven.'

4

Gemma slipped her key into the deadlock on the front door, relieved to be home.

It had been a frustrating first day back at work, a day that had slid by with her mind focused on the image of Kane Fenton and his unwanted appearance in her life, instead of her job.

The journey home in the cold and dark had been a struggle and, somehow, an unsurprising end to a rotten day. First the Underground had broken down, then she had either just missed buses or the ones that had crawled past were full to over-flowing.

And so she had walked home, arriving over an hour late, cold, hungry and weary, and with her mind still troubled.

Only the porch was illuminated when she stepped indoors. The house was quiet, unwelcoming and a bit cold.

Gemma flicked the switches for the hall and landing lights, then went upstairs to her bedroom to shed her work suit before going along to the bathroom.

She stepped under the warm spray from the shower, easing her muscles and enjoying the relief of the cold from her body. With a sigh, she tipped her face to the water. Less than twenty-four hours now before her 'date' with Kane.

Gemma stifled a groan and turned off the water, praying for a miracle. Perhaps he would fail to turn up or he might ring to say they would forget the idea after all. However forlorn the hope, she clung to the glimmer of it.

On Tuesdays and Thursdays, she usually went to the gym for aerobics or circuit training, but she could not face the thought of going back out tonight. Instead, when she left the shower, she dressed in a pair of warm pyjamas, and with her face clean of make-up, her hair loose and damp at the ends, she padded back downstairs.

From the sight of the damp coat draped haphazardly over the banister and the sound of muted thumps and boxes being searched, Gemma discovered that Suzy had arrived home.

She winced at a particularly loud thud that shook the light fitting, and the curse that followed it. Goodness only knew what Suzy was up to now, Gemma thought as she went to the kitchen, her smile a mix of indulgence and exasperation.

A short while later, with a mug of steaming soup and a plate of bread and butter, Gemma went into the sitting-room.

It was warm and cosy, and she offered a silent thank you that Suzy had thought to turn on the fire that glowed its welcome from the hearth.

Gemma crossed to close the curtains, shutting out the muted glow of the streetlights and the flickering veil of snowflakes that billowed down from an unseen sky to form a powdery carpet on the icy ground. It was eerily quiet and deserted outside.

Pleased to put the bleak picture behind her, Gemma curled into her favourite armchair and cradled her mug in her hands. It was bliss to relax, she admitted with a sigh of contentment.

A quiet evening in and an early night would do wonders for her, she was certain.

Her peace lasted a scant ten minutes before Suzy burst into the room, a triumphant smile on her face.

'Found it,' she announced, waving aloft a video cassette.

Gemma picked up a piece of bread and sent her friend an enquiring glance.

'Found what?'

'A film of Kane's I taped a few years ago. I knew I still had it somewhere!' She slipped the cassette into the machine, then sprawled out on the sofa, the remote control clutched in one hand. 'We can watch it together now.'

'Suzy, I don't — '

'Come on, Gem, it'll be fun! There's

nothing else on TV, and it's a foul night for going out,' she added with an irrepressible smile.

As the titles began to roll, Suzy jumped up to turn on a table lamp and switch off the room's main lights, making the room more intimate and atmospheric.

With a sigh of resignation, Gemma curled into a more comfortable position in her chair as Suzy returned to the sofa and turned up the volume on the TV.

The last thing she needed tonight was an hour or two of Kane Fenton's brooding good looks and sultry voice, Gemma thought with a flash of irritation as the film began.

It was one she had not seen before, one from early in his career. He was more mature now, and even more handsome if that were possible. She attempted to concentrate on the plot, a tale of a boy from the wrong side of the tracks making good after the Second World War, but she was distracted by Kane, by his voice, those dark, mesmerising eyes.

Despite her desire to get up and walk away from the film, she found she couldn't. Kane's performance was compelling and she stuck with it to the end.

She couldn't get him out of her head, Gemma realised with annoyance as she lay in bed late that night unable to sleep.

His performance was mesmerising, even though he'd been young when he made it.

Angry with herself, Gemma turned over for the umpteenth time and thumped the pillow back into shape.

This was ridiculous. She had never lain awake stewing over Andrew this way. She banished the traitorous thought. This situation was completely different.

She was concerned about tomorrow night, that was all. More than anything she wished she could call a halt to this charade with Kane. How could she look at him across a dinner table knowing she hadn't stopped thinking about him.

Gemma lay on her side and watched flakes of snow billow down past her window. She knew so little about Kane, she realised now. Despite his success and his popularity he had escaped the attentions of the tabloid Press.

There had been no scandals, no controversies, no tantrums — at least none she could remember. He had been discreet, a loner, keeping his private life separate from his working, public life in a way many people in his position envied.

His reputation as an actor and now as a director and writer was unsullied, and he had gained the respect of his peers and the public. Other than that, she knew nothing of Kane.

Only that he was single despite the efforts of women across the globe to capture his attention.

So with all those women falling over him, why on earth was he taking part in this silly plan?

What his motives were, Gemma was at a loss to understand. And just what would he expect? Being his companion, however much a front it was, was not a rôle she felt comfortable playing.

Troubled, Gemma shifted on to her back and wriggled under the duvet. She wanted to sleep, needed to sleep.

But that would only bring tomorrow closer, and tomorrow she had to face Kane.

* * *

A dark frown hovered on Kane's brow as he left the production offices he had at the studios and crossed the slushy forecourt to his car.

The air was cold, and although the light drizzle that had fallen for most of the day and turned the overnight snow to a wet mess had stopped, a mist lingered, throwing ghostly shadows into the dark of the late afternoon.

Kane snapped on his seatbelt, started the engine and backed out of his parking space.

It was incredibly cold and as he drove

slowly through the studio lot, he turned up the heating, hoping the warming air would soon take the chill from the car's interior.

The day that should have been filled with activity and the building excitement in the company associated with putting a new project in motion had been shadowed with frustration and annoyance.

His initial meeting with his permanent staff had not gone as well as he had planned, and one problem after another had dogged him since his arrival in the office.

His secretary, who had been with him for the last few years, had maintained a watching brief. She had coped admirably with his moods, his insistence on perfection, his punishing work schedule and long hours. What had thrown her today were his bouts of forgetfulness and his apparent preoccupation.

His brief smile faded as he acknowledged the cause of his uncharacteristic lack of sharpness and efficiency. However unwilling he was to admit it, thoughts of Gemma Armstrong were solely responsible. He was usually single-minded and controlled, but he had allowed her unwanted intrusion to affect him and his work.

For the thousandth time since Monday he berated himself for giving in to the impulse to see her again. Why was he involving himself with her quest to lure some man who had to be blind if he hadn't noticed her already?

Richard had told him little about this Andrew person Gemma was so keen on. Only that, in Richard's opinion, however intellectual and presentable Andrew was, he was too cold for Gemma. So why was Gemma so smitten? From the dreary itinerary she had recited to him, he could understand Richard's opinion.

Going out into London tonight didn't appeal to him, especially to what he had heard was one of the dullest restaurants in town. And the prospect of dogging Andrew's footsteps to his list of favourite haunts in the next few weeks was depressing.

He approached his cottage, the car's headlights passing briefly over the river, a shadowed mirage through the trees that stood silent and stripped of their leaves on the bank.

Indoors, he grimaced at the time, and foregoing a drink, he went upstairs to shower.

The warm spray helped clear his head. Dressed and ready to leave, he felt more in control.

He would have this one dinner with Gemma, he decided, and he would satisfy himself that his mind had been playing tricks on him and she was nothing special after all. And definitely not worth the trouble he was causing himself.

Then he would make his apologies, tell her how busy he was, and that would be that. It was only what he should have done at the outset, he allowed. He had made the initial mistake in arranging to see her again, but it was not the end of the world. Even Kane Fenton was allowed to make one mistake.

5

Gemma glanced up from applying the finishing touches to her make-up and watched as Suzy came into the room and flopped on her stomach across Gemma's bed.

'You're not wearing that, are you?'

'What's wrong with it?'

'Nothing, if you were going to some prissy business dinner. For goodness' sake, Gemma, you're going out with Kane Fenton!'

Gemma sighed and turned back to the mirror.

'Please don't remind me.' She checked the clip that held her hair neatly in place, then touched a few dabs of perfume to her pulse points.

'You make it sound like you're going to the dentist for half a dozen fillings or something,' Suzy teased, a hint of exasperation in her tone.

'I'd rather I was.'

'Gemma!'

At least then she'd be numbed, Gemma thought to herself as she slid her feet into her ankle boots and tied the laces.

She stood up and smoothed down the legs of her charcoal, herringbone trousers.

Suzy rolled to her feet and padded across to the wardrobes.

'At least take off that formal jacket.'

'It's a formal restaurant.'

Suzy ignored her quip and rummaged through her things. With a smile of triumph she turned and held out a cream, angora top.

'Wear this,' she pleaded.

Gemma rolled her eyes and counted a silent ten. Suzy had been fussing round her like an excited mother hen ever since she had arrived home from work. As if her nerves needed any further assistance to tie themselves in knots.

The slightest thought of going out

with Kane had her all churned up inside, so much so that she doubted she would be able to eat a single mouthful of dinner.

And what on earth were they going to talk about? She didn't know the first thing about the movie business, and she didn't want to think about Kane's films because the one last night, had only brought back the feelings she knew she had instantly felt for Kane.

But the bottom line was, they were strangers. Strangers who had been thrust together thanks to one of Suzy's whims, although Kane had been adamant they go along with it, Gemma recalled with an anxious frown.

'Gemma!' Suzy snapped her fingers in front of her face. 'It's time to move, it's nearly seven.'

Recognising the stubborn glint in Suzy's eyes, Gemma shed the trim-cut jacket and put the luxurious-feeling top on instead. In an instant it softened her appearance.

The sound of the doorbell forestalled

further discussions or changes of outfit.

With a grin, Suzy crossed the room and bounded down the stairs, leaving Gemma to collect her bag and her dark grey cashmere coat and follow along at a more sedate pace.

As she walked along the landing, she heard voices in the hall. Suzy's was full of laughter, Kane's as warm and sultry as Gemma remembered. Her nerve ends tingled in response.

Taking in a deep breath and trying to relax, she went down to join them.

Her outward façade almost crumbled when she saw Kane. Dressed in dark trousers and jacket, with a brightly-coloured tie at the collar of his crisp white shirt, he looked overpoweringly handsome. A dark raincoat was draped casually over his shoulder.

Gemma tightened her hold on the banister rail when Kane glanced up and saw her. His dark gaze rested on her in a way that unnerved her.

'Hello, Gemma.'

'Kane . . . ' she murmured, feeling

unbearably awkward and tongue-tied.

For once she was grateful for Suzy's incessant chatter as her friend's uninhibited presence helped smooth over the initial moments of painful uncertainty.

It was obvious Suzy wanted them to stay a bit longer so that she could chat to Kane, but he seemed to be keen to get on his way.

With a few words to Suzy, making her blush and giggle at the same time, he ushered Gemma through the door.

Clearly he had a sense of humour and it was a character trait of Kane's that Gemma came to appreciate on the way to the restaurant. Whether he sensed her unease, or whether he was just being Kane, Gemma had no way of knowing.

Whatever it was, she had not expected to find him so easy to be with. He was intelligent and fun — a winning combination and one that soon dispelled many of the knots that were scrambling her nerves.

By the time they reached the

restaurant Gemma was feeling far more positive about the evening.

She would never have believed she could be this relaxed, Gemma marvelled when their order arrived. Contrary to her earlier doubts, she was even hungry.

'Tell me more about Andrew,' Kane suggested after a few moments of silence.

Gemma glanced up and met Kane's intent gaze.

'What do you want to know about him?'

'How did you two meet?' he asked, reaching for the bottle of wine in the centre of the table. 'At work? Socially?'

'No, nothing like that. Andrew's father and mine have been friends since university days. I've known Andrew all my life.' Seeing a frown cross Kane's face, Gemma forestalled any comment. 'I know what you're thinking.'

'What am I thinking?' Amusement chased away the frown.

'That if we've known each other so long and Andrew still hasn't shown any sign of interest beyond friendship, he isn't likely to now.'

'That doesn't necessarily follow. He may think you feel nothing more for him than that. But it is a possibility you have to face,' Kane agreed topping up their glasses with white wine.

'I already know that. I've lost count of the number of times I've told you this was Suzy's idea. You know I didn't want to do it,' Gemma pointed out with surprising calmness.

'True.' Kane grinned. 'And if you find out he isn't interested in the way you want him to be, what then?'

'I also told you that I don't need a man in my life in order to get by,' she remarked, a wry smile curving her mouth.

'Of course, if you've been close all your lives, perhaps you know too much about each other.'

'What do you mean?'

Kane took a sip of his wine.

'There's no mystery, no spice, no sense of discovery.'

66

Gemma broke the hold of his gaze and returned her attention to her meal as she considered his point.

She understood what he meant. But did it apply in this case? Was Andrew too familiar a fixture in her life, her past, for the kind of relationship she wanted?

The questions were uncomfortable ones. Yet the other people she had been out with had fallen by the wayside because she had held Andrew up as a standard. No-one had measured up to him.

'Richard said something about another woman?'

'Mmm.' Gemma struggled to return her thoughts to the conversation. 'Felicity. Andrew has been keen on her for months but she doesn't seem to be interested. Ironic, isn't it?'

Kane returned her smile.

'You and Suzy were at school together? Were you as unwilling a participant in her teenage pranks as you are in this one?'

67

'On the whole, yes.' Gemma laughed, responding to his teasing and the change of subject. 'We're the best of friends but we couldn't be more different. Suzy has this incredible enthusiasm and I couldn't always keep up with her.'

Kane laughed, a rich and throaty sound that did strange things to Gemma's insides.

'Why did you go to boarding school?' he queried.

For the next few minutes she told him about her upbringing, her father's job, her years living in Hong Kong before she was sent back to England for her education.

He was a good listener and Gemma soon felt embarrassed at the way she had chattered on about herself.

'So your parents weren't around much?'

'Not a lot, particularly in my teens. I became self-reliant and grew up quickly. I'm used to being alone, and I know how to look after myself — in every aspect.'

Kane's expression darkened. 'I know what that's like.'

He murmured so quietly, Gemma almost didn't hear them. Something stirred inside her as she recognised a thread of underlying bitterness in his whispered tone he had not been able to hide.

Curious but trying to sound casual, Gemma asked, 'What was your family like?'

An old, bitter loneliness welled within Kane at Gemma's question.

His family hadn't been close. He was a loner, a part of him closed off from the world.

And yet for so many years, that secret, guarded part of him had yearned for love and acceptance, for a place he felt he belonged.

Until he was three, Kane couldn't really remember anything. Nothing of his mother's native Wales was familiar. They had moved to live in London for his father's work . . . His father. A fist tightened in Kane's stomach.

Cold, distant and uncaring. That was how he remembered the man who had walked out of the house during his sixth birthday party and never come back. Kane had neither seen nor heard from him again. A small cheque had arrived for his mother via a solicitor each month for a few years, then nothing.

Kane remembered feeling that his mother hated his presence in the house from that moment on. Sometimes she went for days without speaking to him or caring for him.

Other times she blamed him for everything; her failed marriage, her hated job as a chambermaid trying to scratch out a living, her increasing periods of depression.

It was a shock to realise he had voiced many of his thoughts aloud. He never spoke about himself, his past, not with anyone. Confused, he focused his gaze on Gemma and saw that the misty blue eyes were filled with gentle compassion.

He searched harder and found no

trace of pity, only understanding. His uncharacteristic behaviour troubled him, and yet he never seemed to do the expected when he was around Gemma Armstrong.

There was much he hadn't told her — except things about his mother's deterioration. It was the skeleton in his closet, the juicy titbit he was determined would remain hidden to the grave. He'd had a good relationship with the Press throughout his career, but if they uncovered his secret they would have a field day.

Kane forced his thoughts to withdraw from the melancholy introspection. He had to be on guard with Gemma before he said anything more he would later regret.

'And your love of the cinema?' Gemma queried. 'When did that start?'

Grateful she had not pressed for more family details, Kane pushed his unfinished meal aside and talked of the only thing he had ever felt really passionate about in his life.

'Very early on I found I could escape my own world and lose myself in books and films,' he explained, glancing at Gemma as she nodded her understanding. 'It was a magical, fantasy world and I could lose myself in the lives of others even just for a short time. The adventure, the drama captivated me.'

He took another drink of his wine and a reminiscent smile curved his mouth.

'Every Saturday morning I would be at the cinema, my hard-earned pocket money clutched in my palm. I saved everything for books, movie magazines and trips to the pictures. At school I got involved in all the plays I could, and read all the classics.'

'And then?' Gemma prompted softly.

'I wrote to actors I admired, pestered people for advice and opportunities, worked behind the scenes at the local cinema. Anything I could think of. I was determined that one day I would be in that business. It was all I ever wanted.'

Kane experienced an unusual embarrassment as he confessed those inner feelings that had been so important to him. Gemma's misty blue gaze never left his face, and her silent acceptance spurred him on.

'I started to hang around the studios making a pest of myself. Then I began to be given odd jobs, spots as an extra, or I'd help the cameramen and technicians and learn what went on behind the scenes.'

'Then you were discovered?'

'Not really.' He smiled, watching her as she propped her elbows on the table and rested her chin in her hands. She was really interested and actually listening to him, he realised with a dart of surprise. 'There was a great deal of hard work and a lot of disappointments before I made the breakthrough as an actor.'

'And then you gave it all up to write and direct,' Gemma observed.

Kane shrugged, wondering how to explain.

'Have you ever worked so hard for something and then when you achieve it you find you don't want it anymore, or that it leads you off at a tangent to something different and unexpected?'

'I can understand what you mean,' she allowed with a frown of consideration that amused him. He was intrigued when a faint tinge of colour washed her creamy skin. 'So you'll never act again?'

'I never say never.' He smiled, warmed by the answering curve of her mouth. 'But I don't see the possibility at the moment. I'm excited by the things I'm doing and — '

He broke off as Gemma's gaze strayed past him and her smile widened. Glancing over his shoulder, he saw a tall, blond man walking towards them. Could this possibly be Andrew?

Kane felt an inexplicable tightening of his body as the other man drew closer. He sensed the change in Gemma as she sat across from him, alert and nervous.

This was what they were here for, Kane chastised himself. He had no reason, no right, to feel what he was feeling as he watched Gemma greet the blond man and return his light kiss. He clenched his fists tightly in his lap.

He could not forget he was seeing Gemma for the sole purpose of speeding her into the arms of this man.

That Gemma wanted Andrew had been something he had known from the beginning — it was why they had met, after all. He had just never imagined he would feel so jealous about it.

No emotional involvement, he had assured himself when he had persuaded Gemma to go along with Suzy's plan. A mocking laugh bubbled inside him but he fought it down. He had been fooling himself from the first moment he had set eyes on her.

He, who never had feelings for anything but his work, had allowed his emotions to become involved with Gemma Armstrong in a way he had never wanted nor expected them to be.

6

'Why do you keep insisting there is nothing to tell? You were out with Kane Fenton, in case you'd forgotten.'

Suzy's question greeted Gemma when they met for a pizza after work on Friday evening. She had been fending off her friend's determined interrogation since Wednesday night, but the barrage had continued unabated.

'Because it's true,' Gemma parried, hooking the strap of her handbag over the back of a chair and sitting down.

'There must be more,' Suzy demanded with a frustrated sigh. 'You haven't said anything. What did you talk about? What was Kane like to go out with?'

'Suzy, I didn't 'go out' with him. We had dinner, I came home. End of story.'

'Come on!' Suzy's eyes widened in disbelief. 'I'm not falling for that.'

'It's true.' Gemma shrugged and remained cool.

'Well, what happened when Kane and Andrew met?'

'Not a lot.'

'Why won't you just tell me,' Suzy complained.

Gemma glanced up and hid a smile at the vexed expression on her friend's impish face.

'Have you ordered?'

'Yes,' Suzy muttered with a touch of grumpiness. She slumped back in her chair and pouted. 'Gemma, you are so infuriating.'

A waitress delivered their drinks — and an enormous pizza. Gemma's tastebuds tingled at the scent and the sight of the melted cheese. She helped herself to a slice after Suzy and wiped her fingers on a paper napkin.

'So, is the man of the moment working tonight?' she asked, knowing that the only way to divert Suzy's attention was to mention the firefighter boyfriend who had kept her in raptures for the last three months.

Suzy swallowed the bait as Gemma had known she would. As Suzy chatted happily between mouthfuls about Brian and related the latest stories from the fire station, Gemma's mind wandered back to Wednesday night, and more specifically to Kane.

So far all her efforts to put thoughts of Kane from her mind had proved unsuccessful.

He'd had an alarming effect on her from the start, Gemma acknowledged with a frown, so much so that she had even forgotten why she had been having dinner with him until Andrew had arrived at their table.

The two men had been polite yet cool with each other when she had introduced them. Andrew had recognised Kane and had been surprised to see them together.

His expression had registered a brotherly concern and curiosity that irritated Gemma even now. And how to explain Kane's reaction? Gemma's frown deepened.

His manner had altered, albeit subtly, and the only explanation she could offer for his reserve and air of tension was that he was playing his part of supposed partner far too well.

Yet even after Andrew had rejoined his colleagues for their working dinner, Kane had been more preoccupied and less approachable than before.

The change in him had upset her relaxation and her nerves, and she wondered what she'd done wrong.

Now, as she finished off her slice of pizza and half-listened to Suzy, she remembered what Kane had told her of his childhood. It sounded awful, and she wondered what else had gone on.

That he had told her as much as he had appeared to surprise him as well as her.

There was a loneliness about Kane, she realised thinking back to the conversation they had had over dinner.

He was a successful, highly-admired figure, renowned the world over, and yet she had not imagined the unexpected vulnerability, the inner isolation and unforgotten hurt that she had glimpsed through the outer layers of his veneer.

Perhaps it was her imagination, but for a brief time on Wednesday night, she felt she'd had a glimpse of the Kane Fenton that the public never saw. A man whose inner pain had been skilfully hidden and camouflaged but never healed.

Kane had continued to occupy her thoughts over the next few days. She thought not only of him, but also of the sad, lonely childhood he had had to endure.

It troubled her that she worried so much about it. After all, as she told herself time and again, Kane was nothing more than a brief and passing acquaintance.

Where did they go from here? Gemma was confused and uncertain. Sitting in his car outside the house after their dinner she had felt awkward, unsure of the etiquette for their sort of arrangement.

Kane had said he would phone her, but so far, she had not heard from him. Perhaps he was having second thoughts and didn't want to go on with the plan. She ignored the flicker of regret the possibility caused.

Aware of Suzy's speculative gaze and that her story was coming to an end, Gemma pushed her thoughts to the back of her mind and concentrated on her friend.

She even managed to laugh at the punchline, relieved Suzy appeared unaware of her preoccupation.

'I don't think I could manage any more.' Suzy grinned as she pushed the last remains of the pizza aside. 'You haven't eaten much.'

'I'm not all that hungry.'

Suzy's eyes sparkled with mischief.

'And who is it causing this loss of appetite, I wonder? I mean, you've certainly got a choice these days!'

Gemma bowed her head, hoping

Suzy wouldn't notice the slight blush across her cheeks.

'Oh, stop it, Suzy — that's all you think about these days. Come on. We'll pay our bill and do you still want to go to the cinema?'

'Definitely! And I suppose you already know that they're still showing Kane's latest offering?' Suzy sent her friend a sly look.

'All right then.' Gemma sighed heavily, reaching for her bag. 'I don't suppose I'm going to get any peace until I give in, am I?'

'Absolutely right!' Suzy giggled, a smile of triumph lighting up her face.

Meanwhile, for the thousandth time since meeting Gemma Armstrong, Kane questioned his sanity. He had thrown himself into his work in the two days since he had seen her . . . and Andrew.

It was no doubt lack of sleep that was making him so grouchy and out of sorts, he decided. He'd only had four hours in the last two nights and it wasn't enough. But that had a lot to do with Gemma being constantly in his head.

Only dogged self-control and avid concentration on meetings and preparations for his new venture had kept thoughts of her at bay. But who was he trying to kid? He doubted if five minutes passed at a stretch without him thinking of her. She was just there, all the time, and there was nothing he could do.

Telling Gemma about his childhood had also opened old wounds. He had dwelled more than usual on his past since Wednesday night's admissions, on his absent father whose face he could barely remember, and on his mother.

Kane shook his head and sighed. His mother. She had occupied his thoughts far too much recently.

The ringing of the telephone was a welcome interruption. He swung away from the flickering monitor screen of the computer and reached out a hand for the receiver.

'Hello?'

'Kane, it's Richard. I'd like to talk some more about your proposal.'

'You're interested?' Kane felt his mood lift considerably.

'Very much so.'

'Great. When do you want to meet?'

'I'd like to keep it quiet at the moment. How about a game of squash tomorrow morning and some lunch?'

'Sounds fine,' Kane agreed, his mind buzzing on the package he could offer to tempt Richard's acceptance. He reached for a slip of paper and a pen. 'Name the time and place.'

Just as Kane was about to say goodbye, Richard began to speak again.

'Did you sort something out with Gemma in the end?'

Kane's insides knotted at the sound of her name.

'More or less,' he hedged.

'She's a great girl. Deserves better than Andrew.' There was a pause that increased Kane's tension.

'I certainly can't disagree with you there.'

'But that's women for you! Listen, I'll see you tomorrow.'

'Until tomorrow.' Kane sighed and replaced the phone.

So far he had held back from ringing Gemma again until he could bring some sense to the situation — a situation of his own making, he acknowledged with a self-deprecating grimace.

He could not forget why he was seeing her.

If he went on with this crazy scheme, he had to keep his distance, and the sooner it was over with and he could put Gemma Armstrong out of his life, the better. Picking up the phone, he dialled her number, deflated when there was no reply.

Angry with himself, Kane switched off the computer, rose to his feet and headed out of his study. The house was dark and quiet as he went up the stairs.

An early night would do him good

and he wouldn't think about Gemma. Time enough to worry about his state of mind tomorrow.

★   ★   ★

Self-conscious, Gemma stuffed a wad of damp hankies into her coat pocket and blinked as the lights came up in the cinema. Beside her, Suzy sniffed then blew her nose.

They sat for a moment, reluctant to move, a state that appeared to grip the other people in the auditorium as well.

Gemma felt as if her emotions had been through the wringer. The tear-jerking drama could pull even the most cynical heartstring, and the rustling of tissues, sniffs and muted sobs would have been funny if she had not been fighting her own tears for the last couple of hours.

Gemma felt a swelling of pride in Kane's work. It was a sensational film, one that deserved all the glowing reviews it had already received and the awards that would undoubtedly follow. If he had this kind of talent and vision, she could see why he had chosen to concentrate on this aspect of his craft.

As she and Suzy made their way home in awed silence, each lost in their own thoughts, Gemma thought how strange it was that Kane should have made such an insightful piece about families given his own background. Where did that understanding and perception come from? Or was he still living through his characters a life he had never known?

Gemma was still preoccupied with the film as she sat in the kitchen and enjoyed a late and leisurely breakfast with Suzy the next morning. When the front doorbell rang, her heart almost leaped out of her chest.

Suzy slid from her stool at the breakfast counter and jogged out of the room. After a moment, Gemma heard the sound of Brian's voice and dark mutterings from the hall, an exclamation of surprise from Suzy, then voices muted as the front door banged shut. Gemma, back to the kitchen door, cradled her mug of coffee in her hands.

'Good morning, gorgeous,' she greeted as she heard Brian's footsteps behind her.

' 'Morning, Gemma.'

She nearly choked on her drink at the sound of Kane's amused voice. Eyes wide with embarrassment, she spun round on the stool, her startled gaze taking in Kane's imposing figure then looking beyond him. In the doorway, wrapped around a smiling Brian, Suzy giggled.

Gemma felt a self-conscious flush warm her cheeks. Dressed only in well-worn pyjamas, her hair was unbrushed and her face free of make-up. Mortified, she swept her hands through her hair in an attempt to smooth it out.

When she glanced up, her face clashed with Kane's. The mocha-coloured eyes shone with suppressed laughter and above, one dark brow was raised in teasing query.

'Kane.' Gemma found her voice and steadied it with mild reproach. 'This is a surprise.'

'Sorry,' he murmured, clearly unrepentant, the smile still curving his mouth.

With evident reluctance, Suzy wriggled from Brian's embrace and crossed to the kettle on the worktop.

'Would you like coffee, Kane?' she invited, making the introductions and waving the two men to vacant stools.

Gemma managed to contain a rush of protests. She glanced at Brian as he passed her, bestowing on her a cheeky wink. Tall and athletic with mid-brown hair and deep blue eyes, he had a wicked sense of humour and had more than his fair share of good looks.

With their zest of life, Suzy and Brian were like two peas in a pod. They had been dating for three months, fitting their social lives around his shifts. Their happiness and deepening feelings were clear for all to see. Also clear, Gemma realised with an annoyed frown, was that Brian was unfazed by Kane's presence. Suzy had obviously kept him up to date with her latest master plan.

Feeling tense and far too aware of Kane so close to her, Gemma avoided his gaze and stared with unnecessary concentration at the coffee in her mug.

With an effort, she attempted to relax and join in the light conversation.

When Brian and Suzy rose and announced they were going out for the day, Gemma's tension returned.

She did not want to be left here alone with Kane. Suzy ignored her pleading glance and went off to fetch her things.

'Suzy and I are going to a new nightclub tonight,' Brian said while he waited. 'Why don't you two join us?'

'Oh, no. I don't — ' Gemma started.

'We'd love to,' Kane cut in, halting her vehement protest.

'Great.' Brian grinned. 'We'll meet back here about eight then?'

'Fine,' Kane agreed.

As Brian and Suzy left, Gemma

stared at Kane in disbelief.

'What on earth do you think you are doing?' she demanded, her heated tone betraying her agitation at the suggestion.

Kane appeared unperturbed. 'I thought I was helping you.'

'Really? And how do you work that one out?'

'Isn't it going to look suspicious if we just keep turning up everywhere Andrew goes? Don't you think we should at least act like a couple?'

Kane watched as Gemma considered his arguments. Here he was again, pressing her onward with Suzy's absurd idea when he knew she was reluctant.

And hadn't he told himself enough times that he was reluctant, too? So why did he keep doing this? Where was the distance he had promised himself?

As he waited, a thoughtful frown knotted her neat brows, and she ran the fingers of one hand through her tousled hair in a vain attempt to restore some order to the sunshine-blonde tresses.

Fresh and natural, still with the glow

of sleep in her clear skin, she looked completely irresistible.

She focused that misty blue gaze on him.

'What do you have in mind exactly?'

If he could have, he would have confessed all at this point — the way he felt about her, how he wanted her to fall out of love with Andrew and in love with him.

'Kane?' Suspicion laced her voice as she pushed him for an answer. 'What do you mean by acting like a couple?'

'Andrew's got the message. We don't want to push it, not too soon. He has to believe, isn't that the idea?'

'I suppose so.'

He noticed the frown was back. Against his better judgement, he over-rode his commonsense once more.

'Then we will start tonight, with Suzy and Brian.' He glanced at his watch, remembered Richard was expecting him, and rose to his feet. Somehow he resisted the impulse to kiss her. Before he could give in, and before she could argue further, he headed for the door. 'I'll be back here at eight.'

For some time after Kane had left, Gemma sat at the breakfast counter, staring into space.

She should have resisted his arguments. This was all getting out of hand, especially the talk of establishing them as a couple. A warm and prickly sensation curled inside her. Just what did Kane have in mind when he declared they would start tonight? Start what?

7

The next three weeks sped by and Gemma soon discovered what Kane had meant about them appearing more as a couple.

He dismissed her initial resistance, and three or four times each week they had been out, sometimes with Suzy and Brian, sometimes to places where Andrew would see them, sometimes on their own, once to a film awards dinner.

To her consternation, Gemma found herself looking forward to their time together.

Being with Kane proved to be much more fun than she would have expected and she had even been thinking less about Andrew than usual, a realisation that had made her feel strangely guilty.

Now, a Monday lunchtime, they were wandering round a city centre gallery. Kane looked bored.

She had to admit, to herself if not to him, that the pieces of work they were viewing were not exactly to her taste.

Kane halted in front of an unidentifiable sculpture and glanced at her.

'Do you really like this sort of stuff?' he asked, thrusting his hands into his trouser pockets.

'Don't you?'

'Not my taste, Gemma. Sorry.' The expression in his mocha-brown eyes was assessing and sharp. 'And Andrew really enjoys this?'

'Yes. Yes he does.'

From the beginning, Kane had been cool about Andrew, and although he never said much, she sensed he did not like him. Not that Kane's endorsement was important, she assured herself. She knew her own feelings and it didn't matter what anyone else thought. Or did it? A slight frown knotted her brow.

'Of course, you can see just what the sculptor was getting at, Gemma.'

Kane's over-loud voice and exaggerated accent gained her attention. She glanced at the disembodied exhibit before her, then back at Kane.

'Pardon?'

'Yes, it's the expression, you see. Rich and evocative. And the use of form and space,' Kane went on, warming to the theme. 'Quite a remarkable work, don't you think?'

Conscious that people had begun to look at them, Gemma grabbed his arm and pulled him away.

'Sssh!' She giggled.

Kane was a lot of fun. Andrew was so serious about all this and often in the past had mocked her conservative attitudes and her enjoyment of what he called picture postcard painting.

She liked a lot of the more popular artists. Andrew said there was no challenge, but she could not understand what pleasure was to be had from a lot of the more modern works.

Kane slid his arm companionably round her shoulders and halted her in front of another exhibit.

'Wonderful!'

'What is it?' she whispered, stifling another giggle.

'Gemma, really!' he exclaimed in mock horror. 'You are such a Philistine. Surely you can understand what the artist is trying to explain?'

'Stop it!' she chided, laughing up at him.

He smiled down at her for a moment, then something changed in his eyes, something that made her completely aware of him, of his closeness, of the feel of his arm around her.

Her laughter died. It wasn't necessary for him to look at her like that — far less necessary for her to react to it.

When she made to pull away, Kane held the lapels of her jacket in his hands and stopped her. Nervous, she looked up at him, eyes wide with concern.

'Kane?'

As Gemma breathed his name, Kane pulled her closer.

'Play along. Andrew's just appeared,' he murmured, giving her no time to protest before he bent his head to hers.

The initial pressure of his mouth appeared to take her by surprise. He felt her stiffen, her body tense in his hold as he slid an arm around her waist under her jacket, her mouth resistant to him. Then, after only a few seconds, she seemed to melt into him.

He felt her surrender and he responded to it in a way that would have troubled him if he had been able to concentrate and focus on anything but Gemma.

His hand burrowed into her hair. It felt like silk against his skin. He closed his eyes and breathed in the subtle yet intoxicating fragrance of her.

A stern cough nearby made him start, and with a jerk of surprise, he dragged himself away from Gemma and stepped back a pace. He had forgotten where they were, forgotten he had only meant to put on a display for Andrew.

Kane forced himself to ignore Gemma's stunned expression, the flush that washed her cheeks as Andrew approached.

He also had to ignore the fact that it had been too long since he had kissed a woman and meant it.

Quite when this had become more than a charade, another part he was playing, Kane was not sure, but he, who never let anyone close to him, had allowed Gemma to pierce his defences.

Gemma was not sure how she muddled through the brief minutes they spoke with Andrew. She could not remember a single word of the conversation.

All she could think about was the way Kane had kissed her. Worse, the way she had responded to him. And in front of Andrew.

Thankful to escape, confused and embarrassed, she hurried away as soon as she was able, fixing her gaze away from Kane as they passed a sculpture of two figures locked together in an embrace. She wanted no reminders whatsoever of what had taken place between Kane and herself.

The Thames looked grey under a heavy sky as Gemma hurried along Millbank. She heard Kane call her name, but she did not turn or slow her pace, but he soon caught her up and closed his hand on her arm.

'What did you think you were doing in there?' she demanded as she swung to face him, the wind whipping her hair across her face.

'I thought I was doing what you wanted — to be all over you.'

Gemma drew in a ragged breath, unwilling to admit how rattled she still was from Kane's deeply passionate kiss.

'I don't think there's any need to get carried away. You said yourself that Andrew had the message now.'

Amusement gleamed in the mocha-brown eyes.

'If you're referring to the kiss, why does it bother you so much?' he queried, taking the strands of hair from her face and tucking them back.

Gemma pushed his hand away and gazed unseeing at the river. She realised with embarrassment and inner alarm that her protests were too late and too strident.

Kane may no longer grace the silver screen, but she could not forget that he was playing a part. The consummate actor, this meant nothing at all to him, and it was ridiculous for her to be so upset over it.

'I'm sorry.' She looked up at him and managed a smile. 'You're right. It was nothing.'

★ ★ ★

How could Gemma say it was nothing, Kane fumed when he got home that night. She had to be the best actress in the world if that kiss was just a show for Andrew. She had felt nothing?

It had rocked his senses and sent the blood thundering through his veins, and she said it was nothing.

He muttered darkly under his breath

and went back to his study. His usual refuge.

He would immerse himself in work and forget all about Gemma Armstrong, he vowed, cursing the day he had met her.

Things were moving along apace with his new project. Richard had managed to take holiday owing in lieu of notice and was currently working well with the company. And already he was using his skills to secure the necessary financing.

With other work at the planning stage on top of a busy schedule of interviews and functions relating to his film now on general release, Kane was busy. Too busy. And yet Gemma was still in his thoughts.

He had never felt this way over a woman before and he didn't like it. When she had told him her reaction to his film, he had been warmed with her sincerity and praise. But then there wasn't one thing about Gemma that didn't warm him . . .

Kane ran his fingers through his hair in agitated fashion. He was thinking of her — again. He should never have allowed his feelings for her to deepen. She was only interested in Andrew, though the more he saw of him the less Kane understood Gemma's feelings. As if he hadn't enough problems with his own emotions.

Frustrated and annoyed with his inability to put thoughts of her aside for any length of time, Kane pressed the play button on his answer machine.

The first call was Monica, his secretary, with some details that had come in since he had left the studios. The second was a request for his appearance on a TV chat show. It was the third that got his attention and set his nerves on edge.

'Kane.' A familiar female voice greeted him, the Irish accent soft and lilting. 'Please call me urgently.'

★ ★ ★

103

Kane had sounded odd on the phone, Gemma reflected as she worked through her circuits alongside Suzy at the gym.

She told herself that their cancelled arrangements for the next evening were no big deal, that some space away from Kane was an excellent idea. But she couldn't help feeling disappointed nonetheless.

Not for the first time she wondered what had happened to make him rush off so suddenly for the rest of the week. He had been secretive and distant. Not that she would have questioned him, but a flicker of alarm lingered at his manner and uncharacteristic behaviour.

It was over thirty-six hours since he had kissed her and she could still remember how it had felt, how he had tasted, how her heart had thudded wildly against her ribs.

If that was how he had kissed his leading ladies, it was hardly surprising they had all seemed to be queuing up for parts in his films regardless of whether he was acting or directing.

And no matter how much she attempted to convince herself it had been no big deal, she knew it wasn't true.

Andrew had phoned her at work that morning to ask if she and Kane were serious, if she knew what she was doing. The whole idea had been to ruffle him, she acknowledged, but she had been annoyed and a little bit short with him.

Cultured and suave, she had always admired Andrew's sophistication. She had none of his refinement or self-confidence, nor of Suzy's air of bold assurance. Not in her personal life.

At work she exuded professionalism, but with nothing to hide behind, she retreated to shyness.

Often she had longed to be like Suzy, outgoing, a touch outrageous, or to have Andrew's urbanity and savoir-faire. But after being with Kane these last weeks, Andrew had seemed almost fake. She felt guilty at the disloyalty, but for all his looks, did Andrew have any real substance of character? She had thought so. Before Kane.

Lately, she realised with a sigh, her life had become divided into two distinct compartments — before Kane and after Kane.

★ ★ ★

Kane looked at the woman who sat on the other side of the polished coffee table in the functional, plain sitting-room. In all the years he had known her, she had never been anything but understanding, compassionate and supportive. Those qualities were reflected now in her unwavering brown eyes.

Kane rose to his feet and paced across to the small, leaded-light window that overlooked a tidy, tree-fringed garden.

'I don't know what to say, how to thank you, all of you.'

'Kane.' The soft way she said his name had him turning to face her. 'No words are necessary. Aren't we the grateful ones for what you have done for us?'

'I've done very little.'

The woman shook her head and came across to him. Accepting the silent invitation, Kane enfolded the slight but strong body in a hug, drawing her comfort.

Someone was knocking softly on the door and Kane stepped away, smiling at the shy, young nun who entered the room.

'Forgive the interruption, Reverend Mother, but you are needed upstairs.'

Her message delivered, the young nun left as quietly as she had arrived. It was time for him to go, Kane acknowledged, feeling a deep reluctance to leave this place.

Mother Mary Joseph smiled at him.

'You have become such a friend to us, Kane, over the years. We have watched you grow and are proud of your success, of the man you have become. You have nothing to reproach yourself for. Remember that.'

She turned and took a package wrapped in brown paper off a nearby desk and gave it to him.

'These are her things,' she told him softly.

'Thank you.'

Kane took the parcel and held it to his chest. He hadn't expected to feel so much.

To all intents and purposes his mother had left him a long time ago. The fact of her death was a release — for her, her carers, and for him.

'Your mother may have left this world but you both remain in our hearts and our prayers.'

Humbled, as he always was in the presence of this serene and special woman, Kane thanked her.

'I'll keep in touch.'

'Be sure that you do.' She smiled as she showed him to the door. 'We wouldn't want you to be a stranger to us now.'

Out in his car, Kane put the package

that contained his mother's effects on the passenger seat. It seemed meagre remains of a life.

Conscious of the package beside him on the journey home, Kane struggled through the Friday evening traffic, brooding on the quiet funeral, and on the years that had preceded it, how his mother had deteriorated during his early teens until the time serious mental health problems had necessitated her being institutionalised.

Later he had found his mother a place with the nuns. She had been living in a world of her own by then, a world no-one could penetrate.

Each visit was a painful reminder of a lonely childhood, of pain and neglect, the knowledge that he didn't belong.

Each time he saw her, she had deteriorated and he had wondered with inner pain how long it would go on.

Sometimes, too many times, he had wished he could walk away. She never recognised him, never knew he was there. Despite everything, he had been unable to turn his back on her. Only Mother Joseph and the community, the priest and the doctor, had known about his mother, about him.

The house was dark and unwelcoming when he arrived home. He switched on the lights in the living-room, lit the fire, then went to make himself a mug of soup.

A few minutes later, sprawled on the settee, he opened the package. Setting aside his mother's clothes and personal items, he found an old diary.

He opened the cover and discovered the first entries were from the year he was born.

As he began to read, a cold fist closed tight and hard inside him. With each entry, his life shredded, his very self stripped away.

★ ★ ★

When Kane failed to turn up on Saturday evening, Gemma began to worry about him.

He had told her he would phone, but there had been no word of him since his mysterious phone call last Tuesday night, and when she tried to ring his home number, only the answerphone responded.

Disgruntled at his silence and his neglect to tell her of a change of plans, Gemma resigned herself to an early night.

The news that greeted her the next morning did little to raise her spirits. She could see from Suzy's gleeful expression that she was not going to like whatever it was that had happened.

Quite how bad it was she discovered when her friend produced a copy of one of the Sunday tabloids.

There, splashed across two inside pages, was a story about Kane and the mystery woman in his life.

The accompanying pictures showed Kane and herself during their interlude after their charged visit to the gallery.

'Isn't it brilliant?' Suzy exclaimed.

'Wait until Andrew sees this!'

Gemma was horrified.

'No, it isn't brilliant. Suzy, for goodness' sake! What am I going to do?' she gasped, reading the wildly-inaccurate article.

She could not even refute the gossip, she realised with a welling of indignation. The whole ridiculous idea was that they appeared as a couple. Now everyone was privy to her private life. What a mess. This was the very last time she would ever be cajoled or tricked into going along with one of Suzy's schemes. The very last. Although she had to admit, surely not even Suzy imagined this one would turn out to be quite so dramatic.

'Come on, Gemma, it isn't that bad. Most women would be flattered to be linked with Kane.'

'Well, I'm not one of them,' she retorted, not prepared to be mollified.

There was no reply from Kane's number this morning, not even the answerphone.

112

Anxious about Kane and the newspaper article, Gemma decided the only thing to be done was to go to his house.

The Sunday traffic was mercifully light, but even so the taxi ride dragged, especially as the driver recognised her, the newspaper wedged in the console in front of him. Gemma fended his questions as civilly as she could, but she was fit to explode by the time he dropped off at the foot of Kane's driveway.

His car was there which was a good sign. She had never been here before, but she had little interest in her surroundings at that moment as she crunched up the gravel to the front door.

There was no sign of life from the house. The curtains were drawn downstairs and she peered through the letterbox as she rang the bell a second time. Nothing.

She stepped back and considered her options. From the corner of her eye, she thought she saw a curtain twitch, but there was no sign of movement when she turned to the window.

She was about to ring the bell again when she heard the sound of footsteps approaching the door. The lock clicked, the handle turned, then the polished, wooden door swung open.

The Kane who stood before her was unfamiliar. He looked terrible, unshaven, pale, as if he hadn't eaten or slept for too long. Those once-bright eyes were red rimmed. Slowly, they focused on her.

'Gemma . . . '

She couldn't help feeling alarm.

'Kane, what is it? What's happened?' she implored, momentarily confused and wondering if there was any way the article in the morning paper could account for his condition. Of course not, she chastised herself. Fresh worry welled inside her.

He stepped back and gestured for her to enter the house. As he closed the door behind her, he turned to her,

114

and drew her into his arms. His voice was thick, detached, when at last he spoke.

'I've just found out some awful things, Gemma.'

8

Gemma stared out of the motel window at the distant, snow-capped mountains of Wales. From here it looked as if they were dusted with icing sugar.

Fog had halted their journey from London the previous evening. Now, as the pale sun began a lethargic climb into a clearing sky, it would soon be time for them to leave.

Gemma turned her head and glanced through the open door that connected to the adjoining room. Kane was sleeping soundly for the first time in days, and she did not have the heart to wake him.

Poor Kane. She could not begin to imagine what that initial moment of discovery had been like.

That moment when he had read the diary and found out his life was a lie, that Kane Fenton did not exist, that the people he had thought were his parents were not.

Gemma couldn't believe what Kane's mother . . . what Sylvia Fenton, she corrected herself . . . had done. But the confession of a woman tormented by guilt had been laid bare in the pages of the diary.

It seemed a lifetime since that Sunday morning when she had gone to Kane's house and found him like that. Wordlessly he had taken her to the living-room and pressed the diary into her hands.

Sylvia Fenton had been back at home for three days after the stillbirth of her baby boy. She was going out of her mind with grief — all she had ever wanted was a baby of her own and now that chance had been taken away from her.

She hadn't been out of the house since the tragic event, putting off callers and visitors, unable to admit to anyone the tragedy that had occurred. But Sylvia knew she couldn't go on like this for much longer . . .

The passages went on to describe in detail the horrifying events that had followed. On the fourth day, wrapping up well against the cold and to avoid recognition, Sylvia, numb with grief and determination, made her way back to the hospital at a time when she knew all the nursing mothers would be taking a well-earned rest from their tiny charges. Watching the maternity unit carefully, she waited for a quiet moment before entering . . .

What must that poor, young girl, Bronwyn Lloyd, have gone through when the news had been broken to her that her baby was missing? Tears pricked Gemma's eyes. And Sylvia. How could she do what she had done? How could she live with the knowledge that she had stolen another woman's baby?

Of course, there had been a massive search for the baby but technology wasn't as sophisticated as it is today. Not as much hospital security, no security cameras, and no witnesses.

The police had called round, but Sylvia had hidden the baby away, aware door-to-door enquiries would be made and had cleared all traces of a baby having been in the house. At least, until after the police had been. Friends and neighbours had no suspicions — Sylvia told them she had been resting which was why they didn't see her baby straight away. But now they were welcome anytime . . .

Clearly it had taken its toll, first through a confession to her husband, who decided that to tell the police would have been more dangerous than keeping the baby. But unable to live with the knowledge, he had eventually walked out.

Sylvia's relationship with her 'son' wasn't good either. A lonely, hurt boy, she blamed him for the decay of her own life and her conscience. It was no wonder Kane had felt unloved and alone his whole life.

He had been so vulnerable on

Sunday, so confused. Gemma hadn't known how to advise him what to do with his new knowledge. All she had been able to do was support him. It became clear that he wanted to know where he had really come from, and he had accepted her offer of help with an eagerness that almost broke her heart.

She was not sure when exactly it had happened, but she had come to care for Kane. Seeing him hurting had hurt her, too. He had needed someone, had trusted her, and she couldn't let him down.

Come Monday morning, after agonising hours of waiting, it had been an easy task to track Bronwyn down. The diary had given her name, the place, dates — the baby had still had his tag round his wrist. A trip to the Record Office, followed by a couple of phone calls to a Welsh library for information from the relevant voting list, had confirmed that a Bronwyn Lloyd still lived at the same address, a farm with an unpronounceable name.

There had been no question in Gemma's mind of Kane going there alone. Arranging time off at short notice had not been a problem. Gemma had holiday owing, and recompense for a period of overtime she had put in before the turn of the year. Her boss demanded much but was always fair in return.

The only stumbling block to be overcome before their departure on Monday afternoon had been Suzy. She had not been able to tell her the real reason for the trip, and her excitable friend had waved aside reason and come up with some mad idea of her own. Under the circumstances, Gemma let her think what she wanted. Now they were within striking distance.

In a matter of hours, if all went well, Kane would meet Bronwyn, his real mother.

Kane lay still for several moments, refreshed from sleep. Through the open door to the connecting room, he could see Gemma leaning against the window

121

frame, her arms folded across her chest, her head tilted to one side as she gazed outside.

A pale shaft of sunlight flickered through the dusty pane of glass and fired lights in her silky blonde hair.

She was so lovely. He couldn't believe how supportive she had been. He could have done this alone, of course he could, just as he had done everything alone all his life. But it felt good to have her with him.

Why, when he kept people at a distance, he should trust Gemma so implicitly, he didn't know. She just seemed to reach some place deep inside him, a place never touched before.

He had seen the newspaper she had discarded after she had arrived at his house, and he knew the item about them had upset her. Yet she had pushed it aside, just as she had put her own life aside to be here with him. She was a special woman . . . who was in love with someone else.

Kane smothered a curse and flung

back the blankets. He showered and dressed, and when he emerged, Gemma was still lost in thought by the window of her room. She did not even hear him when he tapped on the door and crossed to her.

★   ★   ★

How serious had Kane ever been about a woman, Gemma wondered as she watched the clouds scud across the sky. As far as she could see, he had always been alone, had never let anyone close to the real Kane, the lonely Kane. Had that come about because of Sylvia's treatment of him?

'What are you thinking about?'

Gemma jumped at the sound of Kane's voice so close behind her.

'You startled me.' She laughed to excuse her sudden breathlessness.

'Thanks for coming with me, Gemma.'

His breath was warm against her cheek. Gemma swallowed and sucked in a necessary lungful of air before she made a determined effort to step away from him, he was standing far too close for comfort.

'I'm glad if it helps.' She smiled.

'You know it does. I wouldn't talk about this with anyone else.'

His words caused her heart to squeeze and her smile to tighten.

'Well, you know what they say. It's often easier to take the ear of a stranger,' she responded briskly.

Kane gave her an odd look, and she dragged her gaze from his. Denying him the opportunity of a reply, she picked up her bag and walked towards the door.

'I'll go and see about some breakfast before we leave. I'm starving.'

Two hours later, feeling a bit more balanced, Gemma closed the map and glanced across at Kane. He was staring at the weathered, wooden sign bearing the name of the farm that was fixed to one of the brick gateposts. The car idled in neutral and Kane's fingers began to tap a disjointed rhythm on the steering-wheel.

'Kane?'

He turned to look at her and let out a heavy sigh.

'Am I doing the right thing? What if this isn't her? What if she doesn't want to see me? What if by doing this I'm spoiling the life she has now?' He looked back at the gateway and dragged his fingers through his hair.

'Life is full of 'what ifs', Kane.'

'But am I being selfish?'

Gemma met his troubled gaze. Reaching out, she laid a hand on his arm.

'I can't tell you what to do. Only that you won't know anything unless you try.'

They drove down the bumpy track, stopping once to get through a five-barred gate. The house came into view, long and low, white-washed with a red door and window frames. Smoke curled from two chimneys set into the slate roof.

The outbuildings that surrounded a small yard off to one side looked functional but not in the best state of repair. Life, she was sure, was hard on these hillside sheep farms.

Kane switched off the engine.

'I'm nervous,' he admitted with a self-conscious smile, his hand hesitating on the door handle.

'I know.' She smiled back at him, wishing she could make this easier. 'I'll let you go on.'

'No. Come with me. Please?'

Gemma glanced at the house then back at him.

'OK.'

They crossed the muddy track to the front door. When Kane hesitated again, Gemma reached past him and rapped the solid, brass knocker.

The woman who opened the door was tall and slender. Her dark brown hair was swept back in a pony tail, a few fine grey strands the only evidence of the passing of the years.

She looked warm and vital, Kane

thought in that first instant. Something locked inside his chest. This was his mother.

He felt Gemma beside him and reached for her hand, thankful to receive a supportive squeeze.

The woman, his mother, wiped her hands on a tea towel tucked in the waistband of a serviceable pair of jeans and sent him an enquiring smile. Recognition of the celebrity lit her wide hazel eyes.

As if she sensed that he was frozen, Gemma took over, making the introductions.

'I'm Gemma Armstrong. I think you recognised Kane?' He saw the answering nod. 'We're sorry for the intrusion, but are you Bronwyn Lloyd?'

'Yes, I am. How may I help you?'

Kane absorbed the gentle, up and down cadence of her voice.

'We have something we would like to discuss with you,' Gemma elaborated. 'If we may.'

Kane watched the surprise cross the

hazel eyes, then she collected herself.

'Of course. Would you like to come in?'

'Thank you.'

Kane felt Gemma's hand nudge him in the back, and he forced his legs into action, crossing the threshold into the cramped but welcoming house. He let go of Gemma's hand and followed down the narrow corridor to a warm and lived-in kitchen.

He was invited to sit, and managed to do so with some semblance of co-ordination. Watching Bronwyn Lloyd as she poured some coffee, he felt swamped with overpowering emotions.

This was his mother. He had been deprived of her as she had been of him through the selfish and dangerous act of the woman who had raised him.

'Now.' Bronwyn smiled as she joined them at the table. 'What is this all about?'

Kane sucked in a breath and struggled to find his voice.

'I think you are my mother.'

Bronwyn's face paled and shock registered in her eyes and the sudden shake of her hands. Wondering why he'd put it like that, Kane cast an anxious glance at Gemma.

'I'm sorry,' he exclaimed in a rush of contrition. 'I didn't mean to blurt it out like that.'

For several moments the older woman remained silent. Kane's tension increased a hundredfold before she finally looked at him, tears evident in her eyes.

'What makes you think so?' she finally asked, her voice huskier than before.

His hand tightened on the diary he had slipped into his pocket.

'I think you had better read this,' he murmured as he drew the volume out and slid it across the table towards her.

9

'I can't quite describe the way I felt when they told me you had gone missing.' Bronwyn wept as she closed the diary. 'I kept desperately hoping that one of the nurses had taken you for a walk round the hospital but that morning soon turned into a day, then into a week, then months had gone by and there was still no trace of you. But I never gave up hope of seeing you again one day . . . '

Kane went round the table and kneeled on the floor beside her, holding her in his arms as she sobbed out her anger and pain at the deprivation of her child.

'Kane,' she whispered, laying her hand against his cheek.

Her touch felt good to him. He pulled up a chair and sat beside her, holding her work-roughened hand in his.

'What happened to you afterwards?' he asked as her tears dried.

'I went home to live with my parents — here, this farm where I grew up. I was very depressed for a time,' she admitted sadly.

'And my father?'

'Dafydd.' A smile curved her mouth chasing away some of the clouds. 'He was devastated also. We had a rocky patch for a while afterwards, but we married three years later.'

Kane threw a surprised glance towards Gemma who sat silent at the table watching them.

'I'm sorry, I didn't realise . . . The surname in the diary?'

'Dafydd is a Lloyd, too! It's a common name,' she teased. 'For a while he worked in the mines and we had a house in town, but the industry suffered, his health suffered, and when my parents retired to the coast, we took over this place. The mountain air has done us good.'

'So my father is here?' he queried,

holding his breath for her reply.

'He'll be in for lunch in an hour, Kane,' she promised, brushing away fresh tears.

'And my grandparents. Are they still alive?'

'My parents and your father's father. You have a whole family here, Kane. We had other children, three girls, and we have two grandchildren.'

Kane found it hard to take in all at once.

'So I have sisters, and I'm an uncle?' He laughed.

'Yes. Oh, Kane, I can't believe this is true. We have never forgotten our precious first baby,' she told him, crying again as she embraced him. 'You look so like your father, you have his eyes, his nose.' She took a hanky from her pocket and blew her nose.

'Oh dear! I have so many questions. I know of you from the newspapers and magazines, but tell me about yourself, your childhood. What has your life been like?'

The initial hurdles overcome, Gemma slipped away and let herself out of the back door, leaving them to talk and get to know one another.

It had been so moving seeing them together, finding each other. She hadn't known whether to laugh or cry, and had ended up doing both. Kane's face at the moment of his mother's acceptance was something she would never forget, his hope, his disbelief, his joy. She was so happy for him.

She thought back to the morning, to his words that he would only have shared with her.

Wrapping her coat around her, she leaned against the stone wall surrounding the yard and sighed. She had assumed it was because she was just passing through his life, not touching it, that she would not be a part of it for much longer.

He had nothing to fear, no reason to assume anyone he worked with or any of his friends would find out unless he chose to tell them. That she was such a transient acquaintance hurt now as the realisation of it had hurt back at the motel.

Despondent, she turned and walked through the concrete yard finding shelter from the cutting wind amongst the buildings. To her delight, she found a warm stable with a few orphan lambs inside nestling under an infrared lamp.

They looked so soft and cuddly curled up in a sleeping mass of wool and skinny limbs.

She wondered what kind of man Kane would be now if he had grown up here with a loving family. Would he still have had a career in films? Or had the emotional deprivations that had driven him to seek some escape from his bleak and lonely existence been necessary for the foundation of that talent and career?

From what she had seen and heard, Bronwyn and Dafydd had survived life's knocks and been brought together by the hardships they had faced. Life here would be a struggle, she was certain, but it was never shallow, and they would never be lonely, as long as they had each other.

'Gemma?' Kane called.

She pushed herself away from the stable door and walked back across the yard to meet him.

'Did you get on all right?' she asked with a smile.

Kane walked right up to her and enfolded her in a tight embrace. After a brief moment of resistance, she leaned into him, enjoying far too much his warmth and his strength. It was good to share in his happiness.

'This is all too good to be true,' he declared with a bemused smile as he drew back, cupping her face and dropping a light kiss on her cheek. 'Thank you, Gemma.'

She shook her head, not trusting herself to speak as she fought an unexpected and unexplained rush of tears.

Stunned, she forced herself to step away and put some distance between them. What was happening to her?

Any time soon this interlude in her life would be over and she just hoped she would survive it. If only she had never been persuaded to go along with this ridiculous plan to win over Andrew.

Pushing her personal confusion and dissatisfaction aside, she walked back to the welcoming warmth of the kitchen where, prepared by Bronwyn, Dafydd waited to greet his lost son.

* * *

This had been the most extraordinary few days of his life, Kane reflected as he drove back to London, Gemma asleep beside him.

Bronwyn and Dafydd — he hadn't known what to call them and they had settled on Christian names as something they were all at ease with — had insisted that they stay a night or two. At short notice, they had assembled the rest of the family, Kane's grandparents, sisters, brothers-in-law and his baby niece and nephew, and held a celebration party.

They had all known of the lost child, and all welcomed him with open arms . . . once the initial shock had worn off, he added with a reminiscent grin.

Not that there hadn't been problems to overcome and decisions to be made. The unanimous opinion of the family had been to keep silent while the reality sank in.

Only when their heads were clear again could they think about the decisions to be made.

Kane glanced across at Gemma and resisted the temptation to reach out and brush back a lock of hair that obscured her profile. With a sigh, he glanced back at the road. She had been wonderful.

And last night when they had sat in the kitchen talking after the others had gone, she had helped him sort out the options in his own mind.

He had to come to terms with the past, and with this exciting new family he had found. If the story of the missing baby and his real identity became known, the Press would have a field day. This was one secret that had to be kept for ever.

Other people had to be considered now. Whatever decision was reached would affect not only himself. The ramifications would spread out like ripples across water, changing the lives of innocent people.

'You know the truth, Kane, and so does your real family,' Gemma had said last night. 'What happened was a terrible thing, but you can't undo the past. You are the man you have become no matter what your name, and nothing will change that. If you don't want anyone else to know, then they won't.'

There was anger inside him and a deep regret that he had been deprived of a family who loved him, a childhood that would not have been lonely. But Gemma had been right.

It was a time for looking forward, not back, and he could not do anything that would hurt the Lloyds.

And so he had made his decision. After Gemma had gone upstairs, he had sat for a while in the quiet and homely kitchen, turning Sylvia Fenton's diary over in his hands.

This was the only evidence of a thirty-two-year-old crime, the only written proof of his real identity.

Even now he could feel that wave of inner peace that had gently swelled through him. Reaching out, he had tossed the diary into the fire in the range and watched as it had burned to ashes, wiping out his past and leaving only hope for the future.

A future, he thought now, that would be all the better if Gemma had a place in it. Again his gaze strayed to her, a smile curving his mouth at the way she had tucked her hand under his head.

He tore his gaze away and forced his mind to concentrate on driving and not on the remembered excitement of kissing her. But her interest was in Andrew, not in him. For all her moral support, he had no doubt she would disappear from his life as soon as Andrew woke up and paid her some attention.

Kane's hands clenched on the steering-wheel. How on earth was he going to walk away and leave her to Andrew when the time came? They had grown close over the few weeks they had known each other — or so he had thought.

Perhaps he was completely wrong because Gemma had been strange that morning in the motel, getting the wrong end of the stick entirely when he had said he had only wanted to talk to her about the upheavals in his life.

He could see now that tight look on her face, the brisk way she had dismissed his thanks with that snappy comment about confiding in strangers.

That wasn't what he felt about her at all. He wanted to tell her. He wanted to show her what he felt, what she had come to mean to him. But he hadn't. Not yet.

She had been quiet this morning,

uncommunicative at the start of their journey back to London, finally taking refuge in sleep. A frown creased his brow as he wondered what was wrong. Perhaps she was still fretting about the newspaper story.

He hadn't given much thought to that what with so much going on since, but he knew she had hated the photographs and story about them being splashed across the Sunday tabloid. He would have to talk to her about it.

A short while later he drew up in front of her parents' stucco-fronted house. He switched off the engine then reached out to give her shoulder a gentle shake.

'Gemma. We're here.'

'Mmm?'

He watched as she yawned and stretched, her eyes, misty blue and soft from sleep, opening slowly. Kane sucked in a breath and scrambled out of the car. She joined him on the pavement and took her overnight bag from his hand with a sleepy smile.

'Thanks.' She yawned again. 'Will you come in for a drink?'

Kane glanced at her mouth then forced his gaze away.

'Sure,' he mumbled, taking a grip on his wayward thoughts.

They barely made it inside the front door before Suzy bounded down the stairs a wide grin on her face.

'Well, it's about time you two decided to come home. I was beginning to think you'd eloped!'

Kane allowed what he hoped was an amused smile of indulgence, surprised when Gemma chided her erstwhile friend, an uncharacteristic snap in her voice.

'Don't be silly, Suzy.'

'Sorry!' The impish grin never dimmed. 'It's just as well though because the telephone has been ringing off the hook. Didn't I tell you my plan would work?'

'What are you talking about?' Kane asked before Gemma could speak, a sinking feeling gripping his stomach.

'Andrew, of course! I think it was the newspaper that finally did the trick. He's been pestering me about you and Kane. He wants to take you out to dinner and the theatre tomorrow night. I accepted on your behalf!'

10

It took several moments for Gemma to absorb Suzy's words and their implication. The news delivered, her friend buzzed into the kitchen, then dashed back upstairs with a carton of orange juice.

Catching her breath and fighting the tide of rising anxiety that brought an uncomfortable tension to her insides, Gemma turned to face Kane.

'Well, you got what you wanted,' he observed, the mocha-brown eyes as devoid of expression as the tone of his voice.

'Yes. It's just taken me a bit by surprise.' The smile she offered wasn't returned. 'I'll get those drinks.'

Kane shook his head.

'Don't worry about it now, Gemma. I think I'll head off. I have a lot to catch up on.'

'Of course. If you prefer . . . '

Her words trailed off, tears pricking her eyes as Kane turned towards the front door. She didn't want it to end like this. It was too sudden, too unexpected. How could she just stand here and let him walk away?

'Kane?'

He hesitated in the porch but didn't look back.

'What?'

'I just wanted to say how pleased I am for you at the way things worked out with your family.'

'Thanks.'

'I think you did the right thing, with the diary and everything,' she continued, aware she was babbling to keep him from leaving. She sucked in a breath when he half turned and she met his intense brown gaze. 'I mean, the legal aspect with birth certificates and national insurance numbers, the Press . . . '

She broke off and watched as his lashes lowered to mask his expression.

Why was he acting so strangely?

It was as if he couldn't wait to leave now the objective of capturing Andrew's attention had succeeded.

Hurting and determined not to show it, she struggled for a lightness she did not feel.

'Anyway, thanks for acting your part so well.'

'No problem.' Something dark and dangerous flashed in his eyes for a moment, but was swiftly masked. 'I hope things work out for you, Gemma.'

'You, too.' With an effort, she managed another bright smile. 'Perhaps we can still be friends?'

He looked at her for a long moment.

'Friends? I doubt that, Gemma,' he flashed, a hint of anger in his mocking tone.

Stunned, she remained rooted to the spot as Kane walked out of the house. Clearly he felt he had fulfilled whatever promise he had felt he'd made, and now he was thankful to end their brief association. The pain at his scornful parting words ate her up inside.

He had played his part as potential boyfriend flawlessly, but that was all it had been, another part, another fictional character from his repertoire. Surely she hadn't been foolish enough to imagine anything else? But she had, she realised, she had been just that foolish in coming to care for him as if their relationship had been real.

Suzy's footsteps thudding on the stairs made her pull herself together. She hoped her friend wouldn't interrogate her about her trip. She didn't think she could stand to think about Kane, not at the moment. She forced a smile as Suzy came towards her.

'Hi.' Suzy laughed, hugging her. 'It's good to see you. I'm looking after Brian just now. He's got a bad bout of flu. I rescued him from his own place and said he could stay in the spare room. I hope you don't mind.'

'Of course not. Is he all right?' Gemma asked, sorry for Brian but grateful for Suzy's preoccupation.

'He's fine.' Suzy nodded. 'You know what men are like when they're ill but you and I will catch up later.'

'I'll look forward to it.'

Suzy emerged from the kitchen with a box of paper hankies.

'I'm so excited about you and Andrew. Just think, Gemma, for all your scepticism, things couldn't have turned out better!'

'No,' Gemma murmured to herself as Suzy dashed back upstairs. 'It's exactly what I wanted.'

★   ★   ★

His performance at Gemma's a week ago had been the best of his life, Kane admitted. The way he had wished her well with Andrew and walked away from her as if he hadn't care in the world had to be worth some kind of award.

He still didn't know how he had kept walking. Perhaps it was a simmering anger at her light-hearted invitation for them to remain friends.

148

Being her friend was not at all what he had in mind, and there was no way on this earth he could see her, think of her, even hear her voice when he knew she was with another man.

And she was with Andrew. Richard, amused by the proceedings, had been giving him a running commentary via Suzy on the state of play. He hoped that Richard had taken his silence for disinterest and would stop talking about Gemma and Andrew.

He had known the score from the beginning, and yet he still felt used. Remembering Gemma's breezy words about playing his part so well made him spitting mad. Did she seriously imagine that was all it had been to him?

The worst of it was that he missed her. She had what she wanted, and for her it was over.

He had been nothing to her but a means to an end, a tool to use to gain Andrew Robertson's attention. Even thinking about the man made him boil inside.

'Anything you need before I go?' Monica asked, poking her head around the door of his office.

'Mmm?' He glanced up, a deep frown etched in his face. 'Oh, no thanks, Monica. See you tomorrow.'

His secretary hovered at the threshold.

'Kane, are you sure you're all right?'

'I'm fine,' he lied.

'Of course you are,' Monica said sarcastically.

'Go home, Monica, before I sack you,' he threatened, an unwilling smile curving his mouth and giving lie to his words.

'Don't worry, I'm going!' She rested a hand on her hip before she turned to the door. 'And so should you. Don't you work too late now.'

He ignored her last bossy directive. She had hovered between mother hen and gossip all week, chiding him for his overwork, nagging him about his unexplained absence as if it was her business, and she'd been agog over the story in the paper.

It was a sorry thing when his secretary was so familiar with him she was amazed he may have a private life.

Not that he had, he grimaced. There was no story, no mystery lady, and he had pointed that out in no uncertain terms to Monica and to the half a dozen reporters who had harried him for a few days.

He leaned back in his chair and propped his feet up on the edge of his paper-strewn desk. As for work, it was the only hope he had of keeping his mind off Gemma. Even his weekend trip to Wales to be with his new-found family had backfired on him because it had felt odd to be there, at the farm, without her.

But some of his inner problems had been smoothed at the farm. He enjoyed the journey of discovery learning to share his life with other people, learning all about the lives of his lost family. They had talked for hours.

Setting the past behind him, spending time with Bronwyn and Dafydd, had given him a glimpse of the kind of family closeness he had never known but always yearned for.

It had made him realise that he wanted a family of his own and wanted to build what had been taken away from him all those years ago. And the only woman he had ever met who he could see it happening with was the woman he could never have.

So many times this last week he had thought of things he wanted to tell her, to share with her. He had been about to reach for the phone, or he'd smiled at the thought of hearing her laugh when he saw her next, and then he'd remembered it was never going to happen.

Kane swore under his breath, dropped his feet to the floor and stood up, the force of his actions sending his chair spinning away from the desk. The memory of her was driving him insane.

Gemma Armstrong was not interested in him. How clear did it have to be before he got the message and stopped wasting his time thinking about her and tormenting himself?

It wasn't as if he didn't know other women — couldn't meet other women if he wanted to. Of course he could, he assured himself with a depressing lack of purpose and enthusiasm.

An image of her long, silky-blonde hair and misty blue eyes, of sweet, delicate features and a sunny smile, superimposed themselves on his brain. With a growl of impatience, Kane slammed his office door and crossed the reception area.

Light showed beneath the door of Richard's office, but Kane ignored the presence of his friend and assistant. The last thing he needed right now was to be waylaid and told the latest news in the saga of Gemma's romance with Andrew.

He wished he had never had the brainwave of calling Richard Morris at New Year and taking him on, then none of this would have happened. He wouldn't now be going crazy.

A grim smile crossed his face. He'd had enough of self-pity, enough of playing second fiddle, enough of pining for Gemma like a love-sick schoolboy. He knew what he had to do. His decision made, Kane strode purposefully out into the rain and crossed the puddled Tarmac to his car.

11

'There's been another delivery for you, Gemma! And it's worth seeing, I can tell you.'

Suzy's excited announcement greeted her as she struggled in the front door and shook out her umbrella on the doorstep.

'Gemma!' Suzy exclaimed with mounting impatience. 'Did you hear what I said?'

'I heard.'

With a final glance up at the leaden sky, Gemma folded the umbrella and closed the door. She shrugged out of her raincoat and hung it on a hook in the porch, then glanced at Suzy.

'What is it this time?'

'Roses! And they're just gorgeous! I put them in the kitchen.'

Gemma glanced into the kitchen at the tubs of flowers filling every available worktop and sighed.

'Very nice,' she murmured as she filled the kettle and switched it on.

'Very nice?' Suzy gawked at her in astonishment. 'Are you mad? They're beautiful! Read the card and put me out of my misery.'

With another sigh, Gemma scooped up the small white envelope and drew out a printed card. As with the five cards that had preceded this one, an image of Cupid firing an arrow was embossed in the bottom left corner, a pierced heart in the top right.

She read the printed words.

Gemma, this is my last hope.

'Well?' Suzy all but elbowed her out of the way. 'Let's see.'

Gemma made two cups of tea, left one for Suzy who was still sighing over the flowers, and carried her own mug through to the living-room.

'For goodness' sake, Gemma, what's the matter with you?' Suzy demanded, following her, a trace of disapproval in her voice. 'I wish someone would do this kind of thing for me.'

Gemma kicked the shoes off her aching feet and sprawled on the sofa.

'Nothing's the matter.'

'Oh, come on. I can't believe you're not excited about this. We've been to all this trouble to coax Andrew out of his blinkers, and now you're playing hard to get.'

'I'm not, I — ' Gemma stopped short and said no more.

Suzy glared at her.

'Then why are you stalling him? Why keep putting him off when he rings? I really don't understand you at all. Is this some kind of payback for the years he didn't notice you?'

'Of course not.' Gemma hung on to her temper with difficulty. 'Anyway, I thought you were against me seeing Andrew.'

'Perhaps I was . . . at first. I certainly never imagined him as such a romantic!' Suzy grinned.

Over the last six days had come a series of gifts, all accompanied by a printed message on the cupid-and-heart cards. None of them had been signed.

So far there had been a heart-shaped helium balloon, huge bunches of daffodils, a book of love poems, several dozen pale blue irises, a large chocolate heart wrapped in bright red paper, and now the roses. It didn't take a genius to work out it was building up to some kind of grand finale tomorrow, the seventh day . . . St Valentine's Day.

At first, wary through experience, Gemma had suspected Suzy's involvement. Perhaps she had been trying to hurry things along, especially when she knew Gemma was acting out of sorts where Andrew was concerned.

But Suzy had been genuinely intrigued and excited when the notes and gifts kept arriving.

'So what are you going to do about it?' Suzy pestered, scuffing the toe of one booted foot on the carpet.

'There's nothing I can do, not at the moment.'

'You could ring Andrew for a start.

What happened with you two? I thought things were working out perfectly.'

Gemma closed her eyes and sipped her tea.

'Aren't you supposed to be meeting Brian?' she asked, pointing to the clock.

'Is that the time already?' Suzy squealed. 'It took him ages to get these tickets. He'll kill me if I'm late!'

'Then go. Stop worrying about me.'

After a few moments of frantic scurrying around for her things, the door banged shut on a hasty, shouted farewell. Gemma breathed a shaky sigh to ease some of her tension. It had been so hard stalling Suzy, resisting her determined questioning this last couple of weeks.

She should have been ecstatic when Andrew had asked her out, Gemma acknowledged. It had been the one thing she had wanted for so long. But their first date together had been a disappointment and things had not improved since.

'I'd never noticed how well you had grown up,' Andrew had told her over dinner, the suave and charming smile fixed on his handsome face. 'You know I've always cared about you, Gemma. It took the realisation you might be serious about someone to wake me up.'

Gemma felt the same discomfort now that she had felt then. Andrew's words had sounded fine, but she had the vague idea he was more interested in stopping her being with someone else than any real desire of his own.

Loving Andrew had been safe, she realised. And perhaps the idea of it, the pursuit, had been more entertaining than the reality.

With a frown, she remembered what Kane had said when talking about his career, that when he'd achieved what he had wanted, he discovered he didn't want it at all. Now, too late, she understood exactly what he had meant.

Going out with Andrew had shown her that she felt no more for him than deep affection, the friendship borne of a lifetime's familiarity. He had been an ideal, a dream — and perhaps even a way she had kept the world at bay? It was a discomforting thought.

When Andrew had kissed her it had been pleasant. Nothing more. She had been fooling herself about her feelings, and she could see now with sad clarity, that Andrew was not right for her, nor she for him. There was no spark, no magic, no explosive excitement and fearful awareness . . . not like there was with Kane.

Kane. He was at the centre of all of this. The whole time she was with Andrew she was comparing him with Kane. And Andrew, she admitted with guilt at her disloyalty, just did not measure up.

Thinking about Kane brought a wave of hurt. She had been nothing more than a game to him and the way he had walked away from her so rapidly, scorning her friendship, had wounded and insulted her.

She was angry with him but knew she

had no-one to blame but herself. From the start it had been a tenuous association brought about by Suzy's meddling. It was her own fault she had come to care for him. And despite the hurt and the anger, she missed him so much, longed to hear his voice, see him smile, be touched by that deep and mesmerising gaze, to be kissed by him again. Her body warmed through at the memory of his touch.

So here she was again, wanting a man who didn't want her. Only this time, the love was genuine. She had never felt so miserable, so empty and alone in her life. Kane had taken a part of her with him when he had walked away from her.

Fighting back tears, Gemma rose to her feet and wandered upstairs to shower. Everything was such a mess and she didn't know what to do. She hadn't spoken to Suzy about it. How could she when her friend had championed her quest, landed her with the problem — and when her brother happened to be close to Kane?

Suzy wouldn't mean to, but it was inevitable she would let something slip, and she could not bear the humiliation of Kane finding out how she felt and laughing at her. News of him had been forthcoming once or twice. She'd even heard, through Richard, that he was involved with a new woman. She desperately hoped this was just work-place gossip.

But however futile her longing for Kane, that was no reason to allow the situation with Andrew to drag on. He hadn't understood her need to step back and have some time to think, and she shouldered her share of the responsibility for the row that had marred the last evening they had spent together.

'It's that Kane person, isn't it?' Andrew had accused, bristling with indignation.

Denial had welled within her.

'Of course not.'

'Don't lie to me, Gemma.'

'Don't speak to me as if I'm a child.'

Andrew had sucked in an affronted breath.

'How serious were things between you?'

'I don't think that's any of your business.'

'Of course it's my business. And being in the tabloid Press . . .'

Gemma's hands had balled to fists. She had refused to discuss it with him, just as she had refused to give credence to the inaccurate story when her mother had phoned having received the paper in their far-flung corner of the globe. Her brief and innocent interlude with Kane was too raw to talk about.

'What about you and Felicity?' she had thrown back at Andrew in counter-challenge. 'I thought she was your ideal woman. You seem to have forgotten about her pretty quickly.'

'Felicity is no longer a part of my plans for the future,' Andrew had informed her pompously as if he were discussing a business venture. 'She's set

164

on her career — no plans for marriage and a family.'

'And are those the qualities you are looking for in a woman?'

It had not been fair to judge him like that, and it was out of character for her to have done so.

Her apologies had been sincere and profuse. Tension had lingered between them, however, and she had wanted space.

Andrew had called several times pushing her to meet him, but she had been adamant that she needed a few days to think. Then the gifts and notes had started to arrive.

Showered and snuggled into her pyjamas, Gemma lay on her bed and looked through the cards and gifts she had saved. She echoed Suzy's earlier sentiment that this was unexpected of Andrew. It felt strange that he should now be chasing her and no longer the other way around.

The seventh package was delivered before breakfast the next morning.

Under Suzy's watchful gaze, Gemma opened it to find a hotel room key, the address on the tag, and the now familiar cupid and heart card.

This is where you'll find me.

Suzy, hazel eyes sparkling, whistled through her teeth. 'This is amazing! I wish I could come with you, but Brian and I have plans.'

'I don't know if I'm going to go.'

'What? Gemma, are you crazy? The guy really cares about you. It was what you wanted, and now you don't know if you're going to go?'

Tears stung Gemma's eyes but she blinked them away. Suzy would never know just how crazy she was, she mocked herself as she put the key and card back in the brown paper.

Gemma thought of little else all day. Suzy had muttered darkly for ages, testing her patience, but she realised how odd it must seem from her friend's point of view.

She wished she could just tell her everything, but she couldn't. And if

Suzy came up with another of her schemes, Gemma didn't think she could bear it. That was how she had landed in this fix in the first place.

Should she or shouldn't she go? She swung from one to the other all day, and it was only at the last minute, that she decided she would. The only thing she was now clear about was that she had to tell Andrew she was sorry, that she couldn't be more to him than a friend. She owed him, and herself, that much, however hard it would be for her to say it.

At home, she changed and showered, then hesitated in front of her wardrobe. There were many outfits Andrew would approve of but she discarded them. She would go as herself, not as the person she had tried to be for him, the person he expected her to be.

She selected a pair of jeans and a soft, powder blue top. Her speech rehearsed, she collected her bag and a jacket, and set off for her rendezvous at the hotel with little enthusiasm.

12

By the time she walked through the plush reception area of the renowned and glamorous hotel; Gemma had a severe case of butterflies.

She clutched the security key in her palm — a palm that felt damp with nerves. As she waited by the lifts, fresh anxiety gnawed at her.

Perhaps it would have been better to phone Andrew than to confront him in person. As she hovered in indecision, the lift arrived, and as the doors glided open, she stepped inside before she could change her mind.

Andrew had been to all this trouble, she told herself on the ride upwards, and he deserved an explanation. Leaving it would not make the task easier.

She wavered again when the lift deposited her on the correct floor. Her knees felt decidedly unsteady as she walked down the thickly-carpeted landing to the correct door.

There was no response from within. She allowed several seconds to tick by, but the only sound was the thundering beat of her heart. There was nothing for it. She was here now and would not take the coward's way out.

The key let her in and the door swung open with the faintest creak of a hinge. She stepped inside a small lobby, closed the door, then entered the main room and froze. The breath locked in her throat.

Huge vases of roses, coloured streamers and dancing, heart-shaped balloons decorated the room. Two bottles of the best champagne nestled in a silver bucket packed with ice and supported on a silver stand.

Beside it was a table covered with a pristine white cloth, carved and delicate red candles, and an arrangement of scarlet rosebuds.

Dumbstruck, Gemma wandered round the room examining things,

smelling the sweet and heady scent of the roses, looking at the labels on the bottles of champagne. On the far side of the table was a trolley laden with salmon and salad, a bowl of strawberries, a box of expensive chocolates, and a cake with red icing and formed in the shape of Cupid with his arrow.

She could not believe that Andrew had done anything so original and romantic. But it didn't change the fact that she was here to call off their relationship before things got any worse.

Her heart jumped when she heard a sound behind her. This was it.

'Andrew, I — ' Her words broke off as she turned, stunned to immobility at the sight of the man who leaned against the door.

Kane? Kane had done this, sent all those gifts? For several moments as she stared at him, Gemma was afraid she was hallucinating.

A ripple of awareness ran through her as she gazed at his familiar and exciting face, the enigmatic eyes, the sensuous mouth, the determined line of his jaw. He looked so handsome and she couldn't believe he was here.

Kane watched in silence as the expression on Gemma's face changed from shock to disbelief. Her initial assumption that she was here to meet Andrew had dealt a crushing blow that almost caused him to turn right around and walk out before he made any more of a fool of himself.

This had been a really ridiculous idea. He could see that now. He should have known he could never replace Andrew in her life.

Somehow he hung on to his composure. He would see it through, he told himself as he straightened and walked across towards her. She looked so beautiful it made his heart turn over in his chest just to see her.

'Surprised?' he asked, struggling to sound breezy.

She nodded back at him, blue eyes wide.

'Disappointed?'

Uncertainty rippled through him as he waited for her answer. He prepared himself for the worst he knew was to come next, and then he saw the tears spill from her lashes.

'No,' she murmured huskily. 'Oh, no, Kane. I'm not disappointed at all.'

He barely had time to brace himself before she threw herself into his arms. Closing her in an embrace that threatened to drive the breath from her body, his relief escaped on a shaky laugh.

He wasn't sure he had ever allowed himself to believe he would hold her again like this, hadn't allowed himself to believe she would turn up this evening, that she would welcome the knowledge it was him.

'I couldn't let you go,' he whispered against her ear, burying his face in her hair. 'I love you, Gemma.'

Fresh tears in her eyes at Kane's husky admission, and the blood coursed through her veins as he laced his fingers in her hair and kissed her with a deep hunger that took her breath away.

When at last they broke a few inches apart, Gemma smiled up at him through the lingering traces of her tears.

'I can't believe you're really here. When you just walked away from me that day and never looked back, I thought it had all been a game to you, that you were pleased to wash your hands of me.'

'No, Gemma.' His hands tightened on her. 'I thought you were in love with Andrew. It was him you wanted, not me. I knew that from the beginning. And I could never have been a platonic friend to you. It would never have been enough.'

'Kane, I've been such an idiot over everything, fooling myself all that time about Andrew, denying what I was feeling for you.'

Gemma met his kiss and returned it, wrapping her arms around him and determined she would never deprive herself of him again.

'I told myself there were two choices — forget you or win you back. So you see,' Kane explained with a smile, 'there was really no choice at all.'

Nestled against him, Gemma looked around the room.

'You did all this? I thought you didn't believe in hearts and flowers and all that kind of thing.' She grinned. 'Kane . . .'

As he opened a bottle of champagne, Gemma watched him, happy, contented, filled with the warmth of love. She took the glass he handed her, but laid a hand on his arm when he picked up a knife and turned to the cake.

'No, don't cut it,' she pleaded, giving him a self-conscious smile when he raised a querying eyebrow.

'I want to keep it.'

'Keep it?' His eyes were laughing.

'Yes. I'm going to put it in the freezer and keep it for ever to remember this incredible day.'

'You're crazy,' he teased her, 'but I love you anyway.'

'Oh, Kane. I love you, too.'

He chinked his glass against hers and smiled.

'Then I propose the first toast. To Cupid, who knows best where to fire his arrows!'

'I'll drink to that!'

Laughing, she did. And when he took the glass from her hand and set it on the table, she melted willingly into his arms.

THE END